Jayne Chilkes, ALCM,  t life
MCAHyp, is an experienced therapist, musician, compo apist.
She has been working in the spiritual field for fourteen years. She has also composed three music tapes for meditation currently selling on the market.

She has worked in the USA and UK, and currently conducts classes and workshops on how to become a spiritual healer and self healing, teaches meditation and the use of sound as a healing tool.

Her path has been very varied from being a secretary to fashion designer, organising and designing her own major shows and opera, running her own shop, writing for newspapers and magazines, modelling and a keyboard player in a band.

Spiritual work gradually changed her life and life-style.

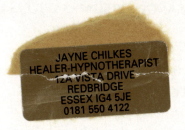

JAYNE CHILKES
HEALER-HYPNOTHERAPIST
12A VISTA DRIVE
REDBRIDGE
ESSEX IG4 5JE
0181 550 4122

Published articles in :
    OVER 21
    ELITE CHIC
    SOHO NEWS
    ID MAGAZINE
    TIME OUT

Book:
    THE CALL OF AN ANGEL

Self Help Tapes:
THE CALL OF AN ANGEL VISUALISATIONS I and II by Jayne Chilkes

Music for Meditation Tapes:
LAND OF POETRY by Jayne Chilkes
INNER KNOWLEDGE by Jayne Chilkes
THE CALL OF AN ANGEL by Jayne Chilkes

Available from:
Bands of Gold, 12a Vista Drive, Redbridge, Essex, IG4 5JE
Tel: 0181 550 4122

THE CALL OF AN ANGEL

JAYNE CHILKES

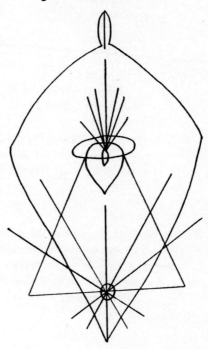

First published in Great Britain 1995
Bands of Gold
12a Vista Drive
Redbridge
Essex IG4 5JE

ISBN 0 9526253 3 4
© Jayne Chilkes 1995

British Library Cataloguing-in-Publication Data
A catalogue record for this book
is available from the British Library.

All rights reserved. No part of this publication may be reproduced by any means, electronic or mechanical, including photocopy or any information storage and retrieval system without permission in writing from the copyright holder.

Typeset in Lucida Casual by the author.
Manufacture coordinated in UK by Booksprint
London, N6 5AH

To Miss Poole
May love and light always be with you
Jayne Chilkes

This book is dedicated with love to all my friends,
friends to be and family -
especially my mother

Thank you to Sue, David, Martyn, and Jonathon for the use of their computer, support and cheese on toast. Also thank you to Vanessa, Pat, Heather, Thelma, Nigel and Simon for their help, love and support. Thank you to you too, the reader, especially for spending your money on this book! Let me know your thoughts...

THE CALL OF AN ANGEL

This is a book to describe my journey to the Light, my path to being a healer, the joys, as well as the trials and tribulations that come with ending Karma. I also include exercises to help you to reach the Light and end your Karma.

I give you the Light
I pour my soul at your feet
I am your servant
We come to deliver you from the darkness
Through this young one's search
You may grow your understanding towards your Truth
and God's Truth
I pray for your soul's deliverance to the Light

I am of a spiritual nature and have not come from one religion. I have trodden this earth many times and believe that I chose to bring God to this planet through my work but I lost my way many times. I have been hidden from God's Light through patterns of my past and ego search for fame, for recognition, to place myself on a pedestal only to be knocked down and bruised, to realise my past life pain which blurred my link to the Light, to realise all my emotional patterns and try and curb them, to understand relationships, to understand human nature, to go to extremes of freedom and of passion, to give healing to hundreds of people, to recognise my talents and build on them, to go where many dare not tread and then find peace, after all battles, in God's Love and Light... I tell you this to have courage, to be totally honest with yourself, to above all love yourself and others and continually fight for your Truth.

"Much of your pain is self-chosen. It is the bitter potion by which the physician within you heals your sick self. Therefore, trust the physician, and drink his remedy in silence and tranquillity. For his hand, though heavy and hard, is guided by the tender hand of the unseen." **Kahlil Gibran**

CONTENTS

PART ONE
Angels Returned
Everyone's a Healer
Extreme Beginnings
A Light Shining in the Dark
First Teachings
Homage to Oscar
Life Lessons
Blessed Meeting
Past Lives
Sirius
Ascension

PART TWO
The Call of an Angel Techniques
Affirmations
First Visualisations
Chakra Visualisations
More Visualisations
Chakras
Sound
Planets and Astrology

PART THREE
When you are a Healer
Return to Love
Further Reading and Courses

PART ONE

ANGELS RETURNED
Channelled Thoughts 1994

We are engaged in an experience to find Truth. An experience that is of earnestness, of purity, of sweetness, of insightfulness, of completion, of beginnings...

A Truth that will show you the Light when the door opens wide and you are home. You are rescued because of that moment of Truth - the moment of completion.

You are in Truth from the essence, the bosom of God. You cannot be from anywhere else because you are that; yet you acknowledge so little of your Truth in terms of the lives many in the West live and adopt as Truth. This is not truthfulness nor honesty but a perpetuation of all that has gone before and no longer holds value.

The value is in the heart, in the essence of your belonging to God's bosom - the word God is used in reference to a higher force beyond your comprehension that guides you in your lessons and learning.
The earnestness comes with the search for Truth - a perpetual task to find that which is right for you, for that moment in time, to bring growth and allow your soul to blossom.

When you find us - the Angels - and others of the same ilk, you know the Truth - the beauty - the wisdom - the love - the honesty - the beingness- you know the planes of existence are reality - we want to talk with you, through you, but only when you are ready to accept such possibilities.

Realignment takes place through meditation especially sounding notes within and around you. This brings our vibration closer to you. You will feel us all around at times, in a group or alone.

Opening your heart and deepening your awareness by meditation is very important. In the aloneness we find togetherness - we spend time and energy in supporting your growth - we produce exquisite patterns in the ether - we cultivate and nourish your growth and understanding - we bring love and constancy to your abode - we place life in your cells - we bring joy to your bodies - we gather up the wounded and bring blessings to their souls - we fight for your lives - we help the Lightworkers make energy patterns for the earth - we rejoice in your development - we are your link between heaven and earth - we rescue you in your darkest moments - we fill you with the hope of light once again - we are your life blood - we are your dearest friends - we serve you as you serve us knowingly or not - you are continually being told to believe in yourselves - believe in this energy - believe in peace on earth once more - believe in after the fall the glory once more - believe in your helpers - believe in your destiny - believe in your emptiness and your fullness - believe in the thoughts that sow beauty or destruction - believe in actions that have cause and effect - believe in new beginnings and new endings - believe in the oneness of all - believe in the fiery storm before the calmness of the waters - believe in Nature as your guide and Earth as your home - believe in Heaven on Earth - believe in non-separation - bring all these thoughts into your everyday environment - your fellow man will know them somewhere for we all originate from the one bosom of God and there we all rest once more, again.

And so to reach these words within yourself you must learn to be an open vessel for God's work. This does not mean there will not be darkness along your path, nor hardship, nor pain, but the Light will forever shine upon your mind to remind you of the faith you have seemingly lost. You have not lost anything nor have you to look very far. It is there always waiting for recognition. We are the Light force that works with all God's children with the purest intention. And know deep within your soul your true intention. Connection to honesty is be developed at every step of the way. And if you fall you must stand up again to walk up the next step and another and another... You can never stand still although it may feel like it.

Rearrange your life if need be to spend time pondering on words of wisdom, on new feelings that come in through meditation or aloneness. Find time to worship Nature again and its gloriousness. To find beauty in all things. To find time to worship yourself, your body, your mind, your path, your decisions, to check out your mood swings, your likes and dislikes.
Find time to wrap yourself in Love.

The pressures of life are all around you especially in the years to come when it seems you will have to give up all the old structures; how this will come about you will see. Land shifts, disasters, economic downfall and who is to help you but those beings and energy forms trying to contact you all the time, to give advice and wisdom.

Your own inner strength and knowing will show you the way. Your trust in the Universe will show you through.

And what of trust? Has it not been written in so many ways over the ages - has it not become embedded in the soul of man - but where has trust gone? Damage has been done and you must return to simple basics of life and living to prepare for a new millennium. You will be constantly bombarded with the effects of disaster and yet you have grown and nurtured them. Let the Light shine amongst the people.

Walk among the people with your Light shining bright. For this is the only way to rebalance the misinterpretation of living. Live in the Light and shine the Light. Correspondingly, the Light will affect some more than others, but it will pierce through even if minutely.

Man has forgotten we share the one Truth - now is the time to re-find this Truth and rebalance our material and spiritual lives. To live withthe Earth and in harmony once more - this is what you must re-find. A new time is ahead of you - let us together bring this forward. And so we will congregate in different sites across the world - we will bless the Earth and radiate Love to its inner structure. We will mend its infrastructure. We will rebalance all the wrong doings of mankind. Those of you who are aware will be our receptors of this energy. You are chosen to spread the Love and Light on an Earth level as we are not of that vibration.

Angel Lightworkers

DAILY MEDITATION - LINKING TO THE LIGHT

You need to find a place in your home that you can make into a small shrine and prayer space. Perhaps a little corner where you can light a candle, have pictures of wise spiritual teachers, crystals or any other spiritual artefacts important to you and an absent healing book.

This should be a place where no-one will intrude or interrupt. You need to find time every day for meditation for at least twenty minutes. It is a good idea to do this at the same time every day.

Close your eyes. Clear your mind as much as possible. Place yourself in a bubble of white light. Fill your body from head to foot with white light pushing out all impurities through the fingertips and toes. Send a prayer for the highest and purest energies to work with you. Send out thoughts for that which you need and give thanks for all the good things in your life. Try to leave all thoughts behind you and dissolve into the white light for 20 minutes. After this time you will find you have much more clarity and know that all answers to questions will be shown to you.

Keep an absent healing book. At the end of the session send out white healing Light and Love to all those people in your book. See them being surrounded by the Light and Love and filled by it. Send the light to specific areas of the person's body if need be. Always end your session by asking for protection with white Light all around you and even put mirrors up around that bubble to bounce away all negative emotions and thoughts from other people in your daily life.

EVERYONE'S A HEALER

In times past we believed in the Guru, the tribal leader, the spiritual teacher - yes, we can have these people as our guiding lights but we can now be allowed to follow and find our own Truth and wisdom. Through meditation every day we can tune into the Universe, God, and spirits who work for God who help us to be the healers and mediums many of us are. Our psychic and healing ability is innate in all of us. Some are more open or advanced than others depending on how much work has already been done on a soul level. Each of our roles are different. There should be no competition or jealousy among spiritually loving people. We should respect each others development and be there to support others to grow.

We are here to make this world a better place. How are we going to do it if we don't keep a check on our lower nature? This includes greed, anger, jealousy, insecurity, fear, lack of confidence, anxiety, negative thinking, hatred, thinking of killing, fighting, lack of respect, feeling unloved, resentful, bullying, laziness, overindulgence, extreme behaviour, being over critical and large ego...

Our lower nature will do its best in whatever form to stop us reaching the Light and being with God consistently. We fall into many traps until we realise what we are doing to ourselves and why.

Firstly, we need to look at our parents, our upbringing and our ancestors, and how they have influenced us. Then, any words said against us or negative situations, personal patterns of behaviour blocking our path and any past life difficulties. Our way of dealing with issues is totally individual. It may be a past life problem before this life. It just depends on the plan of self healing.

Once you recognise problems, find only the best healer, medium, hypnotherapist, astrologer or other qualified person. If you are suffering physically, seek the best possible natural solutions as well as the GP. Search for the spiritual and mental reason for manifesting the illness. There is always a reason but generally we create sickness on a subconscious level. Therefore through hypnotherapy we can contact the subconscious to help us understand and work on the problems concerned.

All takes time. We need endless patience as God and Nature know exactly when we can be allowed to overcome any hurdles in our way. We have to keep working consistently.

We have to give a part of our heart or even all of it, to do God's work. How else will we gain enlightenment? No other way of life will bring long term fulfilment or touch on blissfulness. Being a helper for the Divine can bring the greatest joys.

If you prove sincerely to spirit and God that you wish to help yourself and others in whatever capacity, you will receive gifts beyond your expectations. If you just play at prayer and meditation or psychic work you ultimately kid yourself and maybe badly affect other people too.

EXTREME BEGINNINGS

When teaching congregations of hundreds and thousands you can often be called "successful". That should not impress you. One may be recognised by the whole world and yet be unknown to the only One whose attention matters and he who attracts the notice of God may be entirely unknown to the world. Which would you prefer? Wouldn't you only want the recognition of the Father?

The acclaim of the world can be so intoxicating that man forgets to cultivate the all-fulfilling approval of the Lord.

Eastern Indian

Life threw me in at the deep end many times but I always seemed to be rescued. I wanted to be famous and "success" for ego's sake, seemed to always slip out of my hands as if I was being stopped on purpose.

Please trust your individual process in whatever form that may be, and if my process can help you in any way, so be it...

Seen in its true light, everything is a test.
Trust in your process and know you cannot fail to grow and learn.

"Why did you bring me back?" I asked the angels. I was six years old, staring out of my bedroom window, pressing my face against the glass. I gave the angels a penny and put it by my bed - I prayed to them often.

"Why did you bring me back? Please take me home!" I was twenty-one, hysterically crying, heart-broken over unrequited love, in the College toilets!

I was the only girl in my Foundation Art Class to get into St. Martins School of Art for a Fashion BA Course. I had done something my teachers could not believe. I was accepted into the best Art School in England, but what happened?... Something I had no idea about and no-one around me could help me with. My psychic and healing abilities opened very abruptly - I was talking to guides, and was spouting clairvoyance. I was offering healing through my hands as if everyone understood. I was writing channelled love letters to a fellow student as I felt I knew his soul.

What happened then? No-one supported me - my drawings became beings from another planet and I felt like one too - a complete alien!

The quiet shy me saw a part of myself I had never witnessed before. I felt I was exploding with energy and rebelliousness. I was sent to a psychiatrist (who thought I was fine) and the School Counsellor. I was asked to leave College. I had a nervous breakdown. I wanted to die. I was a failure. I went back home to be cared for. I saw two extremes of self for the first time.

Diary Excerpts 1978-79

"I was on top of the world - I was going to be a famous fashion designer, I had got into the best college in England...

I felt they were my type of people, which I hadn't met for years. I began to see people in a different light, as if they were spirits. It was as if I was in heaven and I knew who was good or bad and aware of things I never saw before. The talent around me made me feel small, though...

I was doing things guided by some other source, like fate, to be at a certain place at a certain time.

Everyone who didn't understand thought I was ill.

The first occurrence of strangeness happened one Sunday at the end of October. I was really excited - over excited that I couldn't sleep all weekend. At about 4.00 in the morning, I had a feeling of someone or many people in my room full of love for me and this strangest feeling of passing over to heaven and I was so full of happiness. I quickly turned on the light and began crying with joy. I began to have visions of the future, some true and some very exaggerated but came true in one form or another."

I forgive everyone
I forgive myself
I forgive all past experience
I am free!

Slowly but surely I bounced back only to move into the most infamous squat in London - Warren Street. A time when Boy George lived around the corner, Steve Strange just opened the Blitz and we "the Elite" (known to the outside world as the Blitz Kids) would dress up wildly and be totally outrageous. Clothes and style were everything - nothing else mattered!

It was an incredibly inspiring time and the ideas for originality and new designs were flowing abundantly. We knew we were an important part of fashion history and all wanted to be famous or were famous!

All was external - we judged ourselves and others only by what they looked like and who they knew. Style was our God. Originality was all that mattered. We competed with each other for the best look. Superficiality reigned.

Deep down, I felt these people were my family and I had known them all before. I had a great deal of love for them and their creativity which was a great inspiration to me and my design work. I was over-flowing with new ideas and found a part of myself I had never seen before. This is the gift given to me amidst the emotional chaos and confusion. And so it is true that every cloud has a silver lining - it just depends how we want to view a situation...

The New Look
Jayne Chilkes 1980

I must wear something new to go to the Blitz this week. I haven't worn anything new for at least two weeks. I mustn't be seen twice in one outfit so I have to change some details to make it look different. She was wearing a scarf draped round her head and I'm never going to do that again. Someone else was wearing shell earrings, I don't feel like wearing mine now, even though they are beautiful.

What colours do I like now? What fabrics? What style? A new look is a definite answer to bring some excitement into my life.

I've decided upon the Eastern appearance using beautiful fabrics, draping effects to the ground. Its something I've never worn before and there is a definite feel in the air. I need matching shoes, headwear and jewellery.

A search around markets, second-hand and Indian shops, a study of books, magazines, museums inspire me. Sketches are made until I am satisfied with the look I have created.

Once the appropriate fabric is bought then the draping can be perfected. I have just received an exquisite Indian headdress of silver and blue - from this my whole outfit will be formed. Using the headdress as the centrepoint all else will be plain, probably an underdress with fine silk draped around me in an appropriate manner.

Gradually my new look is completed. A new me...

We were famous and becoming more so. We went to party and to club and to the "be seen" places. We were allowed in anywhere and everywhere - we were "it"... We appeared in all the magazines and were talked about. There was drink, drugs, sex, bitching and more.

After six months I begun to feel the shallowness, selfishness and loneliness setting in. I saw a medium for a reading who advised me to leave the squat. I didn't understand why she was so worried about me! One day I saw Death as a dark mist walk around the house; I couldn't live there anymore. I knew someone was to die there and I was scared. Sure enough three months later a friend died there of an overdose.

I remember thinking there had to be more than this to life but what is it?...

Diary - February 1981

I sit in my room and cry
As the world passes by
They do not care or try
They only see themselves first
They only hurt
They do not know what love is
Or know how to treat their friend
They only take not give
They are all children

Its not a nice world we live in
I don't suppose it'll change
We have to just accept
Or just sit in our room
Alone...

A LIGHT SHINING IN THE DARK

I am responsible for what I see,
I choose the feelings I experience
and I decide upon the goal I wish to achieve.
And everything that seems to happen to me I ask for,
and receive as I have asked.

In 1981 in the midst of my confusion, I started to realise the true purpose in life and answers to why I was back on this planet.

My friend had told me Elvira would change my life... This was totally true. She was a very talented trance medium and healer. She did not advertise. People found her...

In my first sitting, she said a prayer and apparently disappeared. She transformed into a French nun, Sister Maria. The main message was that my third eye was ready to open. I was not ready before that moment, and I should sit in a development circle. I was overwhelmed and in total awe of the whole sitting and Elvira as I had never come across this phenomena before.

I was then twenty-four, I'd had a nervous breakdown, several very painful relationships, a superficial life-style and friendships, suffered intense physical pain at times and an operation; my time was right and a gift from Heaven appeared. Like a light shining in the dark, a beautiful blessing was bestowed upon me.

I found myself sitting in Elvira's development group. There was a regular group of ten people sitting in a circle. The first night I was petrified. It was something I had only seen on the television as a seance scene. But this was different.

I clung on to my friend's arm as Elvira disappeared again and became Maurice Chevalier singing "Thank Heaven for Little Girls", with a male French accent and tapping her feet He spoke to everyone and had a good giggle. He told me he loved my music! I was not interested in music at that point and understood the comment some years later. It was as if time meant nothing in spirit.

During the evening we were also taught to meditate, send out absent healing and open our awareness to spirit. I loved it. I had come home. I felt I was searching for this all my life but didn't even know. It made a dramatic effect on my consciousness.

We were taught how to control the healing energies, to be patient and take spiritual growth very slowly. As time went on I felt more and more privileged to be in such a loving, supportive and committed group. I was learning compassion, empathy, unconditional love, and how to use healing energies.

Over the five years in the group we spoke to many different people and relations, guides, including White Eagle the door-keeper to the circle; Lily Langtry, a Chinese Sage, Saint John and even Christ. Each time His presence was felt I would burst into tears. The vibration was of such great love, humility and beauty.

FIRST TEACHINGS

The chakras - energy vortexes connected to the body - were used to open up each of us in the group to higher vibrations. Love was the main ingredient and protection was emphasised, especially in closing the chakras down after the session. Slow learning was important to reach higher consciousness and awareness. More learned guides could come through on higher vibrations. We were advised to lose our ego so that the healing energy could pour through us and be passed on to another.

Teachers that spoke through Elvira would tell us that we all have a guide and a guardian angel, and many helpers and teachers can come and go along our spiritual path. We can contact these guides through opening up in the correct way and in some cases become trance mediums where the guide talks through us and we step away. Or, we can be clairaudient where we hear our guide and teachers and then say what we hear. Or just have an awareness of spirit around us helping us. It does not matter which way we work - we are all individual. Some of us become healers, some mediums, and some both. The way to true wisdom is with slow development and working with a good teacher and guidance. Dedication to working for spirit and God must be shown. A part of your heart must be given to doing spiritual work and helping others.

As soon as a soul moves from the physical body to spirit world, it begins a process of awakening. There is no consciousness of time. They may awaken immediately after death and yet by our time measurement it may have been longer. This length of time depends on the state of the person passing over; but usually one who has been interested in spiritual truth quickly awakens to their new life. If they were sick they are placed in hospitals and cared for usually by nuns it is said.

Once ready for learning the most usual way of teaching is to take the soul to the Hall of Records where the soul sees episodes in its life thrown on a cinema screen. No words are said; it is just the truth before the person.

It takes strength and courage to look into the mirror and to see yourself reflected without camouflage; but accompanying this experience comes the teacher in the guise of an acceptable friend who encourages and helps the one who is learning in a gentle and beautiful way. The teacher neither condemns nor chides, but helps the pupil to understand that their life on Earth is the result of former experiences.

Everything in the world of spirit is under the divine law of Love. You are your own judge and own punisher. The suffering you endure on Earth and in spirit is unknowingly self inflicted. Even on Earth if you do something that you know is foolish, the repercussion demonstrates to you how foolish you have been. Spiritual growth is based on the law of sowing and reaping. Yet evolved spirit always stress gentleness and love which governs the operation of this law.

When able to go into the centre of your being, into the very heart of creation, into the centre of life, to the place of quietude and stillness of mind, emotions and body, deep within the centre of your being you realise the true way to act, to love.

Spirit who come from that inner world are aware of the practical details of human life and are not remote from the activities, pains and fears we have. But they love us; therefore they do not remove our problems and difficulties, as this is not kind nor good for us. Spirit stand by our side and give us strength and love while we slowly learn by trial and error. As a result of our dealing with these difficulties, we are moving on the clear path of light and open to the message being brought to us from spirit, we will receive into our souls joy which would be lost to us if they were to remove our problems and difficult-ties. Only we, in companionship with God working in our heart, can experience the heavenly joy of learning these necessary truths. Each time our eyes are opened to the right way of life, each time we are able to touch the secret level of life, the light expands in our heart and soul, and life takes on a new aspect; with our eyes both spiritual and physical, a lovelier view and a more profound beauty than ever, is seen.

From the Source of Life impulses radiate throughout the universe. Permeating all life are these pulsations, these forces, some of which are called positive and others negative. We become a sensitive instrument and through spiritual development and unfoldment we are training to react to these forces in a correct and balanced way, not allowing ourselves to be pulled too much one way or another. We are learning to keep on a steady path of light; to become perfectly balanced souls. A master is a perfectly balanced soul, one who reacts in the right and balanced way to all the influences around him.

All people are linked, consciously or unconsciously, with the Supreme Power, God, and this is why they have the urge to pray for help from an unknown source, a higher power. It is natural even from childhood for us to reach out to something we can love and believe in and respect; and when we grow older, however material and superficial we are, at times of crisis we instinctively call out to God.

All through our life a guiding power watches over us. but it rests with us whether we will act in accordance with that guidance or whether, on the other hand we sway and even work with the darkness. The darkness exists through negative thinking, jealousy, power, fear and hate, and only with our minds. We have the strength of mind not to allow the darkness in. We have the choice. Only the light brings joy, freedom and light.

Anyone ready to respond to the pure selfless influence of a master, sounds a note in the white ether which the master hears and a response comes unfailingly. However, these great ones do not always work in direct contact with us on Earth; they use their disciples and spirit guides to convey their message. We have to be sure that the message comes from a true source. To ring true, it must be of the Christ calibre; it must be pure, selfless, kind and just. In sending us guidance the master will always speak with love, and direct your thoughts towards goodwill and peace; he will never encourage us to antagonism, never to self-aggrandisement, but will always lead us towards humility, loving kindness, and co-operation with our fellow creatures.

A path of progress lies before every soul; every soul has the opportunity to grow in spirit and to give service. When in the spirit world you find yourself in an unpleasant condition you immediately have the opportunity to change, and can quickly progress from limitation or purgatory to a fuller life, and can very quickly rise above limitation into the next sphere of harmony and happiness.

The soul when free meets the loved one on Earth during their sleep normally. Sometimes they make themselves known at other times or through a medium. But during sleep we are being taught how to rise into a higher state of conscious life where we our loved ones and rejoice in reunion.

Souls are not drawn together in physical life unless there is a strong spiritual attraction. It is the attraction of karma; and although conditions between two may sometimes be difficult, any lack of understanding is the result of karma which has to be worked out. It is no use kicking against the painful knocks. The only way to deal with such a situation is to face it and ask yourself what a master would do. Look within and see where the fault lies as well as the fault of the one with whom you have a difficulty.

Spirit want us to understand that their life is interwoven with ours. Our guides and loved ones come close to help us, to lift us up when we are in despair. And when we open ourselves to receive this blessing it brings new life to the physical body. People grow old because of the emotions, the anxieties, the worries they permit themselves; they grow sick through stress and strain. If we always remained attuned to the purest White Light we would not suffer disease.

Spiritual healing is brought about when thoughts are aspiring to the highest force - a Christ-like force. These rays of Light having great power can reverse the order of things; darkness and disease showing in the physical body can be changed; the light takes possession, dominating the body and controlling the physical atoms. Thus miracles are performed. Divine thought arising from a pure and aspiring heart brings the powerful Light.

There are always lessons to be learnt however; there is so much to be learnt by the soul, so much work to be done in a physical body. Earth is like a school, but it is progressive, and as the soul returns in succeeding incarnations it passes all the classes and in due course graduates through the University and becomes a Master.

Spirit want us to understand that every individual soul is linked to another as in a chain, from Earth to the loftiest heights. We can receive advanced messages from a Master. Step by step the message comes down. As spirit speak to us another influence behind them is talking to them to convey certain truths; and behind them there is yet another - and so on through the spheres. Everyone of us with our own guide and guardian angel can be helped beyond all our dreams if we will go with a humble spirit into the inner sanctuary and pray, not in a self-pitying way but humbly; not for self-gratification but that you may fit yourself to be a true servant of humanity.

You have before you the examples of the great ones who have served humanity all through the ages. This is the way of

life, to live not only to enjoy ourselves but to beautify, to benefit Earth, to help forward the spiritual evolution of all life.
The responsibility rests on each one of us.
On the individual soul the whole community depends.

HOMAGE TO OSCAR WILDE
July 1984

He covered me in a veil of love
And reduced my soul to tears and
for that moment we linked as one

Since that time my life has altered
in the most delightful way
A quicker pace of work and play

I'll never know quite how to repay
the love from Oscar Wilde

One evening in Elvira's circle I felt the presence of a spirit. It was male and large in energy form. My solar plexus turned inside out as he tried to come close and talk through me in semi-trance. This was one of my first experiences of such an energy and I was fearful and burst into tears. At the same time, I knew no harm would come to me in such a protected space, but I obviously was nervous of this very new experience.

From then on I questioned Oscar Wilde's presence. I read a lot of his work and biography trying to piece the jigsaw of his life together. For more than three months I felt his presence consistently talking to me, laughing and joking, walking the streets with me and even flirting with my gay friends. I did question his existence and one day I was standing in my shop in Covent Garden, when I almost said aloud "prove to me you are Oscar Wilde!"

The next day I went to buy a sandwich and there in my purse was a farthing dated 1884. This was when Oscar Wilde was just starting his career and even more amazing I found it in the year 1984 - one hundred years difference exactly! It is never heard of to find a farthing in your purse. Where did it come from? I had to take it as proof that Oscar Wilde was walking with me.

Since this time I learnt that spirit try you out and they find it just as hard to come through as it is for you, at times. It can take many years to perfect a good channel and it only happens to a few people who can handle trance mediumship. Our own personal energies can be very drained if we do not protect ourselves and only experience will show us the way. Aiming for the highest quality guide and information is very important and that is why this can take much longer in developing our true purpose. We are all different in vibration and therefore we will never be exactly the same as another medium or healer. Being true to your vibration, you cannot go wrong.

Now as the years have passed spirit do not frighten me in the least as they come close and I absorb the great love that they bring. I have stopped crying if they want to talk through me in semi-trance and I generally only hear them clairaudiently as it is more comfortable for my particular sensitivity.

After fourteen years I am now working consistently with Angels and Light and feel very close to God whilst healing.

CHANNELLED MESSAGE FROM OSCAR WILDE

Society sent me to prison and then into exile. The world that had welcomed me so gladly thrust me out from its care. With the brand of Cain on my brow and the charity of Christ in my heart, I set out to seek my bread in sorrow - and, like Christ or Cain, I found how weary the way was - and, like Dante, how salt the bread when I found it. The world had no place for me. When I walked in public places I was asked to go, and when in hot confusion I retreated, the curious craned their heads or raised their lorgnettes that they might the better view a monster of vice. I had lost everything except my genius. All the precious things that I had gathered about me in my Chelsea home and that had become almost a part of my personality were scattered to the winds or lost or passed in careless and alien hands. The very children of my imagination were thought unworthy to live, and a lady whom I had trusted and who in the days of my pride had often called me her friend, deliberately destroyed a manuscript of mine. As the man was tainted so must his work be tainted also. The leper with his cowl and little bell was not more shunned than I... But though I have forgiven the world the humiliations that were heaped upon me, and though I can forgive even the last insult of posthumous popularity that has been offered me, I find it hard to forgive them for translating my beautiful prose into German. You may smile, but that to the artist was a very real form of murder. To have maimed my soul was terrible but to have maimed the soul of my work was more terrible still. For my work, besides being my great memorial, is my one link with the minds of living men. More than that, it is the golden *thread that will draw me close to the happier generations in the after time...*

Like blind Homer, I am a wanderer. Over the whole world have I wandered, looking for eyes by which I might see. At times it is given me to pierce this strange veil of darkness and through eyes, from which my secret must be forever hidden, gaze once more on the gracious day. I have found sight in the most curious places. Through the eyes out of the dusky face of a Tamal girl I have looked on the tea fields of Ceylon and through the eyes of a wandering Kurd I have seen Ararat and the Yezedes, who worship both God and Satan and who love only snakes and peacocks.

Once on a pleasure steamer on its way to St. Cloud I saw the green waters of the Seine and the lights of Paris, through the vision of a little girl who clung weeping to her mother and wondered why. Ah! those precious moments of sight. They are the stars of my night, the gleaming jewels in my cask of darkness, the priceless guerdon for whose sake I would willingly barter all that fame has brought me, the nectar for which my soul thirsts. Eyes! what can it profit a man if he loses them, or what can a man give in exchange for them? They are fairer than silver, better than seed pearls or many-hued opals. Fine gold may not buy them, neither can they be had for the wishes of kings...

It may surprise you to learn that in this way I have dipped into the works of some of your modern novelists. That is, I have not drawn the whole brew, but tasted the vintage. You have much to learn. Time will ruthlessly prune Mr Wells' fig trees. As for Mr Arnold Bennett, he is the assiduous apprentice to literature, who has conjured so long with the wand of *his master Flaubert that he has really succeeded in persuading himself and other that he has learnt the trick...*

If I may be a little autobiographical, I will go back to the beginning. It seemed to me at first that I had died and passed across the bitter stream to that place of dimness where now I am confined. There was a desolation of the soul that savoured of despair; and yet within me despair had never found a lodgment. I was a fallen god, a fallen king, and felt I had the dignity of royal blood within me. I hardly realised my state. It seemed impossible that beauty had deserted me. I had been condemned - it seemed a monstrosity - condemned by whom? Not by the world, but by a spiteful, narrow crew who could not steer their ship if it fell on a storm. I knew the value of that crew; the knowledge helped me in my impotence. I sat and brooded on the values of the world. Hounded down by little men and called unclean by Pharisees and Philistines I had a greater place in the world's scheme than they had ever dreamed of. This thought brought me a certain quiet. And as day by day came one by one creeping upon each other in sterile dimness, my soul cried aloud that it was healing...

My soul was healing, but my vision of things seen was blind...I wither here in twilight, but I know that I shall rise from it again to ecstasy. The human spirit must pierce to the innermost retreats of good and evil before its consummation is complete...

So, as we enter the spirit world we are the same as when we left the earth plane. We still continue to learn lessons and carry on where we left off. We all have to suffer to learn.

Along your own spiritual path you will find spirits come into your sphere. Some are lost and when you sense this you ask your guides and Light workers to take that spirit to the Light. You see that spirit being taken to the Light in your minds eye. You ask the spirit to leave with Love. You should only work with Light. You learn not to let any spirit into your sphere that is not wanted or appreciated. You are in control and so a rule is never to play around with anything less than the Light. This can have disastrous and frightening results. You must continually pour white Light through your body, mind and soul. Do not work with anything less.

Please work with a spiritual teacher who has your best interests at heart.

Watch out for ego and power over you and those who want the limelight.

Be discerning with mediums and healers. Ask for the highest wisdom and guidance and you shall receive. Be aware of how and where you are developing your spirituality and do not get caught up with anyone or any group that completely take over your mind. Be cautious!

Your action on Earth can reflect the wholeness of Heaven

LIFE LESSONS

*Your joy is your sorrow unmasked
And the selfsame well from which your laughter
rises was oftentimes filled with your tears.
And how else can it be?
The deeper that sorrow carves into your being,
the more joy you can contain...
Some of you say "Joy is greater than sorrow,"
and others say, "Nay, sorrow is the greater."
But I say unto you, they are inseparable.
Together they come, and when one sits alone with you at
your board, remember that the other is asleep upon your
bed.*

*Verily you are suspended like scales between your sorrow
and your joy.
Only when you are empty are you at a
standstill and balanced.
When the treasure-keeper lifts you to weigh
his gold and his silver, needs must your joy or your sorrow
rise or fall.*

Kahlil Gibran - The Prophet

I have listed below Life Lessons that I have tried to learn from my mistakes. Please see visualisations to help you to heal your life further.

- What other people think of you is not important; what you think of is
- What people do not understand they fear
- Only when you love yourself can you truly love others
- Be true to self
- Use your talents - they are gifts from God
- Going to rock bottom makes you want to never go there again
- When the ego is restrained too long it can rebel in unexpected ways
- Failure in man's eyes is not failure in God's
- You can only count true friends on one hand
- When you are opened psychically, in whatever way, be sure to protect yourself and learn to close down and ground properly
- Only tell those who understand the psychic and healing worlds about spiritual experiences at first
- Don't be in love with people just for their talent
- Choose your friends wisely
- People around you are reflections of self
- Don't judge a person by what they look like
- Believe in self and your own intuition
- You make your bed and lie in it
- If you want to play a game you pay a price
- Believe in the Universe looking after and protecting you
- Accept other people for who they are

- You can feel alone amongst hundreds of people
- You are alone but not alone
- Don't take things too personally
- Disrespect of self brings disrespect of others
- Reality is not as beautiful as dreams
- Running away from life is ultimately harmful
- Experience life to the full to know self
- Superficiality breeds superficiality
- No love, no respect; no respect, emptiness; emptiness, no love
- Pain of the heart does heal eventually
- Learn from your mistakes
- Have faith in self
- Follow all your dreams to be fulfilled
- Make opportunities happen
- Be focused and disciplined
- Work from the heart and not the ego
- Believe in your strength and courage

BLESSED MEETING
1986

Elvira had become too ill to run the development group. She moved away. I was devastated as she and spirit promised that I would be working with her and I was too attached to these ideas.

After a while, I began to scream inside for a new teacher. I tried to find one but I just couldn't find a very high standard anywhere...patience on your path is hard to learn!

Well, this time the scream was so loud, the Universe heard me! In walked Graham.

I was invited to a friends house. He sat at the fireplace and some feet away. There were a few others in the room too. Suddenly after ten minutes his presence filled my whole being and I sobbed for half an hour! Nobody in the room could understand what had happened to me.

It was a cleansing for what was to follow...

The room emptied and Graham and I then sat opposite each other for 4 hours and the effect on each other was inexplicable... We had gone to Heaven with our eyes open. We were of the same beginning; we were one and the same. Words have no justice to this meeting.

We spent many evenings over many years working with our amazing spiritual link. His intensity opened my memory to past lives with him and all sorts of spirit guides would come in. I would talk to him as his mother as if in the time of the Essenes. Angels came in, an Egyptian priest with scrolls of knowledge would talk through me - the whole experience was incredible and yet we could not really share it with anyone nor really be understood.

This misunderstanding still goes on today and we have to be careful who we share our spiritual experiences with. Until you are strong in your understanding and more confident, do not tell the whole world of your experiences. Only tell those you can trust - this may only be one or two people - that does not matter.

Diary 23 March 1988

I went "home" last night
Full of wondrousness
Full of adventure
Full of kindness
Full of love
Blessed in courage
Flowed with joy
I went home

I met a friend last night
Of great wisdom
He held out his hands
For my brother to speak
The words were formed
But did not utter
As I gave birth to spiritual matter

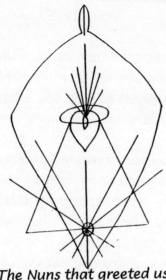

The Nuns that greeted us
Prepared the way
To the noble soul
To follow through his duty
And I gave birth
As I opened my empty vessel
With trust, love and the need
to help somehow

And the aftermath;
Full of questioning
But knowing of all
Simple
Sublime
Speechless

PAST LIVES

The vibrations are now such that we are allowed to see our past lives more easily. We can tap into moments of joy and pain. Use a good hypnotherapist to help you especially if you have a block you do not understand, seemingly coming from another life.

My experiences were again not at all what I expected. Past lives were something I knew nothing about and did not understand. I have now spent many years clearing all the corners of my past lives to be free in soul. It has not been an easy road and I had to find a lot of courage to face some of the pain I was carrying, but the rewards are so great I would recommend all to free themselves.

I started to remember one Egyptian past life with Graham in 1987 but it was too difficult to deal with. In 1991, my close friend had just recovered from a mental breakdown which in fact caused me to look deep inside myself and deal with pain. I knew I was ready to deal with my past life.

I set up a session at the College of Psychic Studies and I was talked through to being in a meadow, relaxing there, and then up a hill and steps leading to a door. (At this point I had not realised this was a very basic hypnotherapy session.) Closing the door firmly behind me I stood in a room with twenty steps down at one end. I was counted down these steps to another door. I opened this door and I stepped through into an Egyptian room setting. I was wearing beautiful clothes seated all alone on a throne-like stone chair with hieroglyphs painted on it and all around me.

I cried very deeply. All my people had gone and I was left alone. I was asked to go back in time and I immediately stopped crying. I saw a male priest of authority telling people what to do. I did not like him and he seemed to cause some sort of war or uprise. A lot was happening but nothing much to verbalise. I felt I was a priestess/healer and I was taken away afterwards to an island like Crete to spend the rest of my unhappy life. It was like watching a sad film but not always understanding the plot or only retaining certain frames.

Although the session seemed complete I was not clear from emotion. The story was not finished and I was running the film continuously in my conscious mind. I was me in the present and someone else in the past - it was very disorienting and disturbing. I prayed that when I went to Totnes I would meet a healer who dealt with past lives. I knew no-one who did this at the time.

Then in Totnes, ten days later, the most extraordinary thing happened. A woman came over and sat beside me in a tearoom. I recognised her from a course we were on three years previously. We chatted for quite a while and then she mumbled that she did past life healing. I could not believe it. I told her everything and that I was feeling very very strange.

She knew it was extremely important to clear me immediately. God had sent me an Angel.

Within an hour we found a healing room and we went to work. What happened was devastatingly painful, emotionally. I needed someone of her vibration to deal with it as she had already had much experience.

It was a perfect healing room with a large tropical plant which filled the room with good energy. I sat beneath it. The woman rubbed my feet first - the Metamorphic Technique. The energies began moving in my body - I closed my eyes - I was feeling anger towards my father, torment about men and then Egypt...

"They burnt everything", I sobbed. I saw the beautiful clothes I was wearing, white turned up shoes, white robe with a panel down the front. I was a woman.

Q.	"What are you doing?"
A.	"I don't know."
Q.	"Was it a secret?"
A.	"Yes it was."
Q.	"Did the people understand you?"
A.	"No!" Then I vaguely said "they burnt everything" sobbing as I saw books and bodies being burnt more clearly. "All the wisdom of my father (who was a teacher) is lost."

I felt left without a soul. The people had gone and all my work had been taken away from me.

The pain was so deep, words could not describe the experience. I held my heart very tightly because of the physical pain. But suddenly the whole atmosphere changed. There was a change of energy as spirit entered and healed my heart.

The woman described it as if my heart was an egg cracked in half. Spirit were giving me my other half - the cracks were being healed. The energy was so powerful. Pink and gold was being poured into my heart. It felt whole again for the first time in my life. That part of me that didn't want to be on this planet in this life was now linked. That part of me that feared the loss of all my spiritual work again was almost gone. My pain was lost.

My memories were faded. The energies poured into my head and body. I felt more whole than ever. It was a mini miracle in my life that I will never forget. I was very fragile for a few days and could not believe what had happened. I couldn't thank the woman enough but as fast as she appeared in my life she disappeared.

Always believe that help is there if you need it. God works in mysterious ways.

Although I thought this was an ending it was only a beginning to many more memories to deal with from other lives. Unfortunately the Egyptian chapter had not closed as a man came into my life who was the soul who took my work away from me due to jealousy on his part. He actually gave me a lot back to support my work in this life, but my journey with him was extremely difficult as I feared and loved him so much and I did not know why. It was a jigsaw puzzle I was allowed to put together eventually and an obsession for seven months.

    He was someone in power in Egypt and I practically kissed his feet. We were very close and even lovers but I wanted to do my spiritual work. He did not like it and he put an end to everything I was trying to do. The story did not end there as I started to remember I was pretty nasty to him in a Greek incarnation. I did not want to continue Karma and so I decided to discuss this with him. We did and I finally cut myself from his influence and his power. It was a very difficult and complicated situation and one I do not wish to repeat. It took a great deal of courage to tell him what had happened to me but I did it. Nothing seems so hard now!

    In the many lifetimes of our existence we can stumble upon circumstances unforeseen and people who wish to inflict pain through jealousy or power. We can attempt to move out of their way or we can stand strong; yet, their influence is so embedded in our soul we are drawn back like a yo-yo. We may find this happen for many lifetimes. When we meet these people again we automatically reflect on a subconscious level and feelings can shoot out of our body and soul. At the time of first meeting there seems to be no rhyme or reason. No whys or wherefores but sometimes a stream of terror and excitement waves through your whole being. And then you fight with all your might to stop this happening but you keep seeing this person to try and understand. It may take days, weeks or months but gradually you can see and feel the links and your mind opens up to the memories of painful encounter with that person.

Along the way, I was supported with extraordinary healings from angelic beings and messages. Elvira talked to me through my friend for two hours and explained what was happening to me and why. My friend was talking about subjects that she had never heard of - it was totally amazing. I had a conservation with Elvira as if I was speaking to a friend normally. It proved yet again how we gain great gifts through facing pain.

Once you have seen the Truth you can decide what to do with the pain - let it go or hold on - you have the choice - go back or go forward. Return or heal the ordeal. Heal lifetimes of anguish in a moment. Heal embedded patterns deep-rooted. You are in command of your own destiny. Find the strength to face such pain and fear. Find the love to pull you through especially with prayer. Find the friends to hold you together and push your way through it with all your will and inner strength. Fight and break the patterns of lifetimes and stand afresh and glowing in Universal Light and Love, free at last.

Unfortunately, I still had more memories to deal with in further relationships. It seemed endless and very intensive until I met another past life friend and lover in 1994. He almost completely cleared me through hypnotherapy and healing every day for a month. I had nothing left. I was in void for six months but knowing my nasty corners were almost clean. We know not what we sow and the web we weave. We are here to grow and learn and look these challenges in the face.

Be brave and be strong. Feel the fear and do it anyway!

SIRIUS

Some American Indian tribes believe they came from Sirius and some believe that whales and dolphins did too. They believe if we have an affinity to whale medicine our DNA understands that sound frequencies can bring up records and memories of ancient knowledge. Whale medicine people are usually clairaudient or able to hear very low or very high frequencies. They can use sounds and frequencies that balance the emotional body and heal the physical form. They can tune into primordial language and when they find the sounds that release the ancient records they can change their outlook on life. In using the voice to open memory they can express their uniqueness and their personal sound.

I was told and feel my first incarnation was in Lemuria. We sung then the tunes of the animals and plant life. All was of beauty and harmony with Nature. Our vibration and awareness then was very different although I believe we are working towards becoming that aware again. As our DNA changes with the forthcoming vibrational changes we will become more of an energy being than human as we know it.

One evening with friends, we felt a different presence which was definitely not a spiritual being as we knew it. My friend described a space man, we felt decidedly weird for three quarters of an hour. It was difficult to understand what they were trying to say but this is the message I received in the end.

SIRIUS VISITORS
8 February 1990

Wisdom is in the echoes of fields of energy.
Remember the force field.
The capacity of flight into space.
We are here waiting for you.
We come to help.
You cannot hear us because you are deaf.
Open your ears and your hearts.
Look into your rainbow.
Your sadness is your own fault. Your happiness is your right.
Blessed are those who hear us.
We fight for your survival.
We seek you out to fight with us.
Listen and cleanse your senses.
We talked to the Egyptians and you will remember.

Suddenly not ever hearing of Sirius before, I was intrigued. Who are these people and what did they mean to me? There aren't too many books on the subject. I found out about the African tribe Dogon beliefs and drawings, and the Egyptians worshipping Sirius which apparently could be seen in the sky then. I also found out that a rainbow has been seen around Sirius in the sky confirming "look into the rainbow" in the message. I sat in classes to reach more of an insight, and then I received messages from the Sirius family for about three months partly about a sound machine I should make but couldn't make it in earthly terms! There was always such a desperation for the Sirius nation to get through and help this doomed planet and I tried my best in my own way to pour energy to the Earth whenever I could with my groups.

EXCERPTS from SIRIUS CHANNELLED MESSAGES
June 1992

We are in a time of great change, disillusionment, demolishing of old structures. We must learn to render ourselves open to receive the wealth of higher knowledge. We cannot be students of life without our fluidity for where are we if we are to stick only to old principles and never let go of habits of a lifetime or many lives. The change is upon us. We have agreed to play our part in this massive evolutionary turning point. We will feel the stirrings and shakiness as others but those of us who are working as helpers in any way may develop the sense of objectivity thus helping many others through this disruptive phase.

We are not alone. Yes, we have spirit guides but also cosmic guidance. The help of a higher intelligence trying to work hand in hand with us - to heal the planets structure and restore harmony and to also heal our auric structure and body harmonies. We are out of alignment as is the planet.

We will become further distressed by what will occur to the planet and we have little time to redeem our past. Mens minds are left fighting for their own greedy motives and still cannot perceive how destructive they have become. These men and women are unlikely to take on board any words of warning but a revaluation will be taken. They may no longer be permitted to destroy much more.

Their motives are the innocents destruction.

The pure in thought must be allowed to shine their Light on the invalids of the 20th century. Harsh but true.

We implore you to work in any way from the heart to help. And thus the rewards are manifold. Peace enters your realm, love penetrates every cell of your body and you begin to link

*with the workers of light of the unseen force.
We come in armies to help you and your planet...*

Reducing waste is our prime motive. Therefore we must find new technology to ensure this. You must conserve, as little is already left. Repeatedly throughout history you have come to this standing still - no way out point. We implore you this time not to destroy and rebuild but to turn history and build up before destruction. This is our reason for being so close at this time to bring new information to you and to cast away doubts and to allow positive action to take over. You must build eliminators to suck away electromagnetic debris in the atmosphere. You must use solar energy. You must find new ways to eliminate body wastage to stop the pollution of waters. You must build gateways for the energy of the universe to be drawn into the earth. These are spiritual and man made. They are shapes to be placed all over the surface at energy cross points to restructure the Earths grid. You must do this now. This will stabilise the planet a little more so you can go forward in your development. The shapes can be small pyramids. Set up a network throughout the world to do this. Planet healers are to go and heal each energy point. Gather in the people...

The Sirius Ra people await the approval of many more humans before they are accepted as being here with us. They search for lifetimes for carriers of their wisdom and truth. They are indeed of great sincerity and great minds. They flow as with the sun on beams of energy between Sirius and the sun. They lead lives of truth and integrity and wish to establish a link with our world. It is time for that link to be known *and to be upheld from millennium of years of working with planet Earth. Recognition is variable over the centuries. They are back because we are being made ready to hear. We are growing into carriers to plant the seeds. The seeds to grow new life, new energy, new abundance that will replace the old way of thinking and provide a better source of nourishment and replenishment for all. They are here to teach us new technology to fend our crops and labour our fields. They are here to re-energise our planet. To feed it with new energy and to teach us of equipment that feeds energy into the planet. To teach us how to conserve energy and not to waste. They talk to minds that can hear. To people who are ready. They are of the sun and solar energy is much of their propulsion. Solar energy is being used slowly more and more. They must teach us how to clear up our mess. They are our teachers and we should welcome them instead of question them. We should open our arms to this new beneficial knowledge pouring through. We are here to be cleared in mind and soul to hear them well. They are indeed searching for new channels daily and they scour our nations to find reliable bearers of truth. They are not interested in false egos nor in false tongues. We await their information in anticipation for their return in full force. This will be a sign of victory and completion of a cycle in history with a new beginning of living in harmony with Universal Law and Nature.*

May that day come soon...

We wish you well. We come with tenderness in our hearts. We know your pain. The loss of friendships dear is not easy but we ask you to bear with it. It is a loosening of old habits. Retaining a power or bond is that which brought you back to the

Earth plane. You do not have to return so learn this well. Love with heart to all but belong to no-one. Place your heart in the hands of Eternal Love and you will see the difference. Your whole being will flow constantly. You will no longer need people to be happy. You will remain with them and love them. The subtle difference is you can let them go and they no longer need to be part of you. You are unto your own - no more fears my child we are with you.

Who are you?

We are the fighters - the ones who help you and many others to pass the light through. We are many and not one. We have banded together to fight with you. We are so truly grateful for your co-operation.

What do you look like?

To ourselves we are shiny metallic. We have hands and feet but bodies of a different energy to yours.

Are you male or female?

We are neither.

How do you mate and re-form?

When it is time for a new born we apply energy to the foetus lying dormant in our womb.

Does every planet have different life forms?

Yes of course. If we numbered them we would talk forever.

Do you believe in God?

God to us is energy. We are all energy and we are all part of it.

Do you feel His Love?

We feel compassion for all. We are enduring and infinitely more regular than humans in our consistency of compassion. We are not linked to emotions in your way. We have to learn tolerance of such things as we do not feel at all in the same way as you. This is something we learn from you.

Have you ever walked on Earth?

Some of us travelled to Earth in other lives and we have traces of earthly conditioning in us.

What was your work in Egypt?

We spoke to you then as we speak to you now. We did not walk the planet. We walked with you. You were similar then as you are now. You remember us and we remember you for your work then. We are teaching you again the many secrets you have forgotten but once knew.

This channelling ceased after three months. It seems that this can happen to many mediums. Energies come and go and so do guides. I found this an exciting time and puzzling. We are all so multi-faceted and so we do not know what is truly hidden in our subconscious.

In the end I found my link to Sirius and I feel my search is over for now. In 1993 I was in Sedona, Arizona - an incredible part of the world - and I received this message unexpectedly:

The first flights that landed here were from Sirius
Dog star people left over from the interstellar conflict -
there was no choice but to bring our people here.
We communed in the mountains - these are landing pads
unused for thousands of years - you are remembering
the peaceful nation - the nation that once were your people -
your family.
You still contribute to the Earth - we had no choice but to
leave you here - you still communicate with us you see.
Blessings upon you - the task at hand is to reduce wastage
especially this area - a major power centre for the Earth -
any abuse here could cause even more disaster.

You are called upon and your people to take heed - spread
your healing light out to this area - reconnect - go home
sense the oneness in your being and spread it out as you
travel your way.
We called you here and you have come. We asked you before
and you are here. Welcome home.
This is the closest proximity to us that you could come to
on this planet. This is your original landing pad - you
were then and still are one of us.

This is the last of the special landing grounds - caress it.
There is nowhere else to look - you have found us
and we are forever with you in your heart.
This was once a city. You lived here amongst our people -
thousands of years ago - not many have come back with you -
you know them when you see them - you helped

build this energy field - we give some back and reunite you -
this is a momentous occasion -
you have not been here for thousands of years in the physical
WELCOME HOME!

The time we talk of is Lemuria/Atlantis time period - between this period. You cultivated the energy through prayer, crystals and machines -
deep underground are your machines
you helped control machines and energy with a link to universal law
a time of advanced learning - reach out and feel
biospheres, stratospheres, luminescent beings with round heads, long hands and feet - living underground - remnants left today.
Keep your knowledge to the few who understand.
The memory lives on even though the people are not here.

~~*~*

I wept buckets all through receiving this message. This was my Truth.

I then had a reading from Dr Peebles and he confirmed that I once lived on Sirius looking for safety, sanctuary and security. Apparently I had to return to Earth still searching!

Just because you believe something does not necessarily mean to say it is true

ASCENSION

Groups have been formed to wait for Ascension and to leave the planet with our cosmic friends. This may be so, for some.

In my experience Ascension is bringing our soul truly in tune with our body and using more and more Light. Our vibration becomes increasingly higher as all our darkness leaves us and we can attain a oneness with soul - Heaven on Earth.

There is no going back at this point. Once this is a constant there is a feeling of Ascension and that perhaps you cannot go any further. Every step we take towards the Light seems the best and truest.

It has been foretold that our DNA structure and our physical bodies are changing back towards being energy beings again in around one thousand years time. We are feeling these changes already. Our chakras are changing, disappearing and moving to different areas. We may get headaches and kidney pains due to the changes in our vibration. The planetary vibration is allowing us to change. It is as if we have travelled full cycle to original form, to oneness with Divine Source.

We all have the right to return to Heaven on Earth. We forget we are beautiful cosmic light beings. We forget everyone else is too.

We can go "home" and be here on planet Earth. We do not have to look far. It lies within our heart. That flickering light that lights us all and links us to Divine Love. We have to take one step at a time to off-load our baggage and pray for the steps up to clear our way to bring us to comfort, peace and joy. Love starts to radiate from every pore. This is when we have a constant smile on our face; when we stop criticising others; when we stop worrying; when we lose all fear; when we love without wanting anything in return; when we clearly feel and see the light in an instant; when the material is in balance with the spiritual.

And when Love walks in, and never leaves us;
when we hear the Call of an Angel...

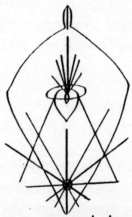

I give you my soul, dear God
I give you my heart
My direction is entrusted in thee
Show me the way to do thine work
I am your Servant, dear Lord
May your blessings run through me
To touch the world

MESSAGE FROM LORD AKHENATON
September 1994

In the image of the Father God who art in heaven we mirror His Excellence. We are mirroring His Divine Presence. We are the Ancients taking refuge in God's Bosom. For unlike many others, we come to rescue you from the Beginning of Time and now we sit on the Highest Throne to bring new wisdom afresh to your people and planet.

Take heed there will be many who do not understand. There will be many who hesitate to come to us. Remember oh, chosen ones, the Light can be too bright for many.

You are chosen at this time for one reason only - you have earnt your place in Heaven's Heart. You no longer have to walk the streets down trodden - you are in the Light. Those who recognise you follow you. Those who do not remain in solitude and in despair.

They are souls to be rescued or left behind. You can but help for a while and then it is their choice. Beckon them, but if they do not follow, let them go immediately. You have done all you can in an instant. Do not linger, there are too many others to rescue willingly.

God bless you.

Lord Akhenaton

I hope that my journey has shown you hope for your path in whichever way that takes. There is always light at the end of the tunnel. May your journey be safe, joyous and above all courageous. May you all find your Light within and spread it wherever you may go.

PART TWO

THE CALL OF AN ANGEL TECHNIQUES

These techniques are formulated from my knowledge of hypnosis, healing and visualisation to help you enter a deeper state of awareness, to know who you are and give you a more abundant and happier life experience.

These techniques help you to have good health, more wealth, achieve your goals, clear negative emotions, help relationship problems, understand your negative patterns of behaviour, open your healing and psychic awareness and in so doing, you in turn help to heal others. You can find you are in touch with your higher self consistently and your guide, teachers, and angels. You can find you are a worker for light and want to do God's work through this process. If you are already on the healing and psychic paths these techniques will still help bring much more clarity and awareness into your life.

Brain Frequencies

Our brain frequency fluctuates countless times every day, completely spontaneously, as the need arises. When we go to sleep at night, and close our eyes, our brain automatically starts cycling down so we can rest, dream, and become rejuvenated. Our sleep process is necessary for us to maintain our mental and physical health and balance.

Beta

When we are awake and performing our daily chores, our brain operates in the beta frequency range. This is from fourteen cycles per second upwards, with most of our activity being at about twenty to twenty-two cycles per second. This is our conscious mind. At this level, we reason, rationalise and do whatever jobs we need to do.

If our brain frequency gets too high, say around sixty cycles per second, we would be in acute hysteria. Much higher than that would probably bring disastrous results, perhaps death.

Alpha

Between seven and fourteen cycles per second is the alpha range of brain activity. This is where day-dreaming and dreaming at night take place. Hypnosis also takes place here.

Theta

Between four and seven cycles per second is the theta state. All our emotional experiences are recorded here. This also is the range from which you can reach into clairvoyance and healing techniques.

Delta

Frequencies less than four cycles per second are encountered in total unconsciousness, the delta state.

Sleep state

When you drift into sleep, your brain quickly cycles out of beta through alpha and theta quite quickly, and into delta for a short while. Typically, we might make the transition from beta into delta in about thirty minutes, then remain in delta for from thirty to ninety minutes. At that point, our brain would cycle up into theta, and into alpha where we would dream for a while, then cycle back down into theta, then up into alpha for more dreaming. In an eight hour sleep period, you might spend thirty to ninety minutes in delta, thirty to sixty in theta, and the rest of the time in alpha.

This is an illustrative sleep cycle. It will vary from person to person, and even from night to night with the same person. The important thing to note is that altered states are a natural phenomena that we all go through every day.

Even when we are awake, we dip into alpha and theta frequently for very brief periods. For instance, if we close a door on our finger, our brain dips into theta to record the pain.

Or perhaps we are studying and trying to memorise some material in theta. We look off into space to record the material in our brain at alpha.

Healing and Psychic Techniques

When we need to reach our psychic and healing ability we are learning how to deliberately cause our brain to go into theta and remain there for as long as we wish without falling asleep.

The following techniques will open the door further for your potential as a healer and psychic, and you need to make an agreement that you use this knowledge to promote only loving, positive, caring thoughts for yourself and others at all times.

Visualisation

The key lies in reaching theta at will and then using that state to achieve healing and psychic experiences - this is the main reason for visualisation.

We use visualisation to help us relax our mind and body deeper and deeper so that we can access the theta frequency for our benefit and for the benefit of mankind, and the planet as a whole. These visualisations begin to disperse any negativity held within our subconscious mind. The subconscious holds all the information and memory of the self from conception until the present and beyond this lifetime. It has been programmed by our environment and our thinking to know right from wrong and can be reprogrammed if necessary to change patterns in our life.

This is the beginning of a special journey into the power of the mind and how you can change your life and fulfil all your ambitions, wishes, create good health and live in abundance in harmony with nature and the world around you. These techniques will act as a catalyst to bring you into joy and true fulfilment for the rest of your life.

AFFIRMATIONS

Affirmations can be then made from any negative experiences. Some useful affirmations are:

- My physical body is a pleasant and wonderful vehicle for my full and free self expression
- My mother and father, family and friends love and appreciate me
- I no longer feel unwanted. The Universe rejoices at my presence in it
- The Universe is singing in my atoms
- I love myself, therefore others love me
- I am willing to accept love and stop resisting
- It is safe to surrender to love
- I always get what I want and I only want good things for me
- I only attract loving, good people
- I no longer suppress my feelings, I express my feelings to others easily
- I forgive myself completely. I am innocent.
- My body is young and healthy and I am healed
- My negative patterns are now dissolving effortlessly
- My past is complete. Everything is resolving itself harmoniously
- All my past relationships are now clearing up easily and pleasurably
- The more self esteem I have the less jealousy I have
- I am a beautiful lovable person, and I deserve love
- Every day and in every way I am more and more able to receive
- All of my relationships are now loving, lasting, and harmonious
- The more beautiful my thoughts are the more beautiful people I attract

⌇EXERCISE TO FIND YOUR OWN AFFIRMATIONS

My most negative thoughts about myself are:

....

....

....

Now turn these negative thoughts such as "I hate my body" to a positive affirmation such as "I love and respect my body" or "I am a wonderful, healthy human being". Then write this affirmation fifty times on a piece of paper. Totally concentrate on writing the affirmation and really mean it. If you feel you do not believe this new affirmation after fifty times you may need to look at why. Write down the reasons why you do not believe this affirmation. Then tear it up and try again. If this does not work you may need help on a deeper subconscious level with hypnotherapy as to why you cannot believe in your new affirmation. Many blocks are revealed in this process. Do not be too hard on yourself but above all be honest.

My new affirmations about myself are:

....

....

....

FIRST VISUALISATIONS

You may find visualisation a problem you can practice as follows:

✧ *Close your eyes and think of an apple. Picture the apple and see the colour or colours of the apple. Then bite into the apple. Taste the apple and feel the texture of it in your mouth. Look at the apple where you have taken a bite. Then slowly open your eyes. See if you feel hungry after this short exercise!*

✧ *Close your eyes and think of a rose. Picture the rose and all its petals. See the colour of the petals. Smell the rose. Place it in a vase. Then slowly open your eyes.*

✧ *Close your eyes and think of your favourite animal. Look at its eyes, ears, nose, and body. Touch the body and feel the texture. Send the animal love. Then slowly open your eyes.*

You are now ready to move on...
  Some basic rules:
*You should complete each of the following basic and chakra visualisations in sequence.
*Only do two a day.
*Try to spread them over a period of a week.
*If at any time you find you are feeling emotionally or mentally blocked just imagine a dustbin liner on your back and fill it with all your fears, anxieties, worries, negative thoughts about yourself and stress. Close your bag tightly and just throw it away into the dustbin and close the lid tight.
  Then you should be ready to do any further meditation or visualisation.

*The Call of an Angel Visualisations I and II tapes are available for all the visualisations but you can make your own from the following scripts.

*Remember to find a place without any interruptions and where you can relax. Find a comfortable chair or bed. If making a tape keep the tape recorder at arms length away from you. You need to make a tape of the words in italic, pause where suggested allowing the tape to continue, speak slowly and clearly. When you have finished the visualisation rewind the tape.

*Make yourself comfortable and turn the tape on to play.

✍VISUALISATION 1

Close your eyes to help your concentration. Breathe into your feet and feel the muscles in your feet - tense your feet and then relax. PAUSE.

Breathe into the muscles of your legs and feel the muscles in your legs - tense your legs and then relax. PAUSE.

Breathe into the muscles of your buttocks and feel the muscles in your buttocks - tense your buttocks and then relax. PAUSE.

Breathe into the muscles of your abdomen and feel the muscles in your abdomen - tense your abdomen and then relax. PAUSE.

Breathe into the muscles of your chest and feel the muscles in your chest - tense your chest and then relax. PAUSE.

Breathe into the muscles of your back and feel the muscles in your back - tense your back and then relax. PAUSE.

Breathe into your neck and shoulders and feel the muscles in your neck and shoulders - tense your neck and shoulders and then relax. PAUSE. Feel the whole body feeling heavier and more and more deeply relaxed. PAUSE.

Now up to the face - screw up the face muscles and then relax them. And now your scalp muscles - tense the scalp muscles and then relax them. PAUSE.

And now all the muscles around your eyes and eyelids - feel them - tense these muscles and relax. PAUSE.

Let all that relaxation pour through from your eyes completely down to the tips of your fingers and toes. PAUSE.

Take another deep breath - relax even more as you imagine you are outside - see the sky above you. PAUSE.

Take another deep breath - relax 10 times more deeply. Now mentally visualise and repeat the number 1 forming in the sky. PAUSE.

Take another deep breath and relax ten times more deeply. Now mentally visualise and repeat the number 2 forming in the sky. PAUSE.

Take another deep breath and relax ten times more deeply. Now mentally visualise and repeat the number 3 forming in the sky. PAUSE.

You are now at the deepest level of consciousness and relaxation that you have ever experienced. Mentally visualise and repeat the number 3. Any time in the future that you mentally visualise and repeat the number 3, you will go as deep as you are now or even deeper.

In the future, all you need to do to reach this level or a deeper level is to close your eyes, take a deep breath, allow yourself to relax, see the sky above you and mentally visualise and repeat the number 1, then visualise and repeat the number 2, then visualise and repeat the number 3. PAUSE.

Take a deep breath now, and go deeper. PAUSE.
Find yourself on a beautiful white cloud protecting you and allowing you to float around with joy and peace all around you. PAUSE for 1 minute.

When you are ready count yourself back from 5 to 1. At one your eyes open and you are wide awake and feeling good about yourself.

You now have the first tools to easily access alpha and then theta more easily and for learning to relax and heal yourself. Now all you have to do is count one, two, three and find yourself in a deep relaxed state.

✧ VISUALISATION 2 - EVEN DEEPER

Close your eyes, step outdoors and see the sky above you.

Take a deep breath and visualise and repeat the number 1 as you exhale. PAUSE.

Take another deep breath and visualise and repeat the number 2 as you exhale. PAUSE.

Take another deep breath and visualise and repeat the number 3 as you exhale. PAUSE.

You have now entered an altered state of consciousness by the 1-2-3 countdown. In the future you will merely be instructed to enter your altered state by the 1-2-3 countdown and you will be expected to perform the 1-2-3 countdown and visualisation by yourself.

Imagine now that you are standing in front of a temple. See your name above the entrance. This is your temple. It is the temple of your mind... of your consciousness. PAUSE. Now walk inside and look around you. You have been here before. This is where you have spent much of your life in the past, living day to day, fighting problems the hard way, winning some, losing some. Beginning now, you intend to start using more and more of your mind. This means opening more doors in your consciousness. This means going to any higher level of consciousness that you wish whenever you wish. Your goal is to enrich your life and the lives of others by more extensive and efficient use of your mind and its innate healing and psychic power. PAUSE.

You see a fountain of white light in the centre of your temple. Bathe in it to cleanse and heal your mind, body and spirit. The white light is full of unconditional love and protection and penetrates every cell of your being. It cleanses your body and aura and you see yourself in a bubble of pure white light.

All darkness with you is pushed away. From now on you are working with the light and take this protective bubble everywhere you travel. PAUSE.

At the other end of the room is a staircase going down of 10 steps. You count as you step down these steps (count slowly and with each breath) 1-2-3-4-5-6-7-8-9-10. You are now at the bottom of the steps. In front of you is a door marked TO THETA. You are now in deepest alpha at the threshold of theta, which is your best awareness level. In the future, whenever you count down from 1 to 3 while visualising and repeating the numbers 1-2-3 you will enter deepest alpha at the threshold of theta just as you are now. The door in front of you leads to theta and into the world of psychic and healing experience. There is a golden key that unlocks this door. In the next session you will return here to open the door and enter into higher awareness. PAUSE.

Now climb the stairs count 10 to 1 on each step. PAUSE. When you are ready count 5 to 1 to bring you back to beta level of consciousness. At 5 you are on the ground floor of your temple, at 4 you walk past the fountain and out of the temple, at 3 you find yourself back in your physical environment, at 2 you feel yourself in your body, and at 1 open your eyes refreshed and wide awake.

If your visualisation is not as clear or vivid as you would like, do not worry. Just perform these exercises to the best of your ability. Your visualisation will improve with practice. Part of the purpose of these exercises is to train your mind to visualise at your command. The next exercises are to work in Theta level in your Room of Enlightenment. This is where you can attune yourself to all your needs, understand your problems, tune into the needs of others, heal yourself and others and set yourself free through positive commands and affirmations. So again play **Visualisations I** or make a tape for the following exercise.

✏️VISUALISATION 3 - YOUR ROOM OF ENLIGHTENMENT

Enter your deepest alpha level in your temple of consciousness by the 1-2-3 method. I will stop talking for a short time while you do this. PAUSE for 1 minute. You are in your temple, you have a bubble of white light around you, and you count 1-10 and you are at the bottom of the 10 stairs. You are now at the deepest alpha level in your temple. There is a door in front of you named TO THETA. PAUSE. Hanging by the door is the golden key. PAUSE. Now reach up and take the key and unlock the door. PAUSE. Push the door open fully. PAUSE. As you walk through the door you step into a rainbow of colours. The colours are the most vivid you have ever seen. You walk into the reds, PAUSE, the oranges, PAUSE, the yellows, PAUSE, the greens, PAUSE, the blues, PAUSE, the violets, PAUSE, the pinks, PAUSE. Then you see the room; your special room of enlightenment. Your bubble of white light and colour now expands and fills the whole room with pure white light. You are free here, free to create, free to be who you are, free to do whatever you want. This light and colour is all knowing and comprises all frequencies and allows you the ability to perform as a channel for any worthwhile purpose. Continue to absorb this light and colour. PAUSE.

Now walk into the centre of the room and create a chair. PAUSE for 10 seconds. Now sit down in your chair and find an all-purpose button on one side of the chair. PAUSE for 6 seconds This button enables you to bring anything you command into or out of your room of enlightenment. To test your button, mentally say "I want a screen in front of me". Allow the screen to descend from the ceiling and appear in front of you where you can use it. PAUSE.

Now say "Go back" and press the button and watch the screen raise up and out of sight. PAUSE You can raise and lower it as you wish. You have absolute control in this room.

Now it is time to attune. Be comfortable in your chair and mentally say "I want my protective bubble with mirrors around it". See it descend from the ceiling and drop over and around you. PAUSE. The energy is transparent and full of light. You can see it vibrating as it attracts positivity. Around the bubble you place mirrors facing outwards. The mirrors deflect any external negativity and cannot penetrate your bubble of positivity and protection. PAUSE.

If you generate harmful negative energy it cannot pass through your bubble and harm others. You must take great care to not generate negative energy because it will remain trapped within your own bubble where you must deal with it. You are learning to deal with your own negative energy by overriding it with positive energy and action. PAUSE.

Now you have found theta you can automatically transport yourself to this level and your room of enlightenment. You need not concern yourself about levels any longer. When in your room you will be instantly adjusted to wherever you need to be. PAUSE. Now take one last look in your room. You like being here. PAUSE

You are now ready to leave your room, close the door behind you, and climb the 10 stairs, counting 10 to 1 as you climb the steps, then 5 to 1 to return to your physical environment.

☞ CHAKRA VISUALISATIONS

Continue to make a tape of each of these visualisations and play them back or buy The Call of an Angel Visualisations I and II.
Sit in meditation and concentrate on your base chakra front and back, breath in the colour red at the base and chant Oh resonating with the base chakra for five minutes.

☞ BASE CHAKRA

Go to your room of enlightenment using the 1-2-3 countdown, followed by the descending staircase while slowly counting 1-10 on each step. I will stop talking while you do this. PAUSE for 1 minute. You are now in your room of enlightenment.

When we enter our room we are here to heal ourselves as well as others. We are here to gather knowledge and information according to our need. We are here to benefit the planet and mankind. We wish no harm to any other person or living thing on this planet or on any other. When we enter our room of enlightenment we replenish our soul and heal our body and mind. We are here to learn and reconnect to higher wisdom to bring this into our conscious daily living. We are here to strengthen our weaknesses and recognise our strengths. We are here to love ourselves as well as others. PAUSE. When I suggest these words please mentally repeat them after me:
I agree to use these methods at this level for the good of all humanity. I can cleanse the base chakra with the colour red and the sound Oh. When I do this I will not develop any illnesses associated with the base chakra such as arthritis or any bone disease or kidney failure. I will always

maintain a perfectly healthy body and mind.

Now, settle into a comfortable position in your chair. PAUSE. Press your control button and allow your screen to descend in front of you. See that screen turn a bright red. PAUSE.

This screen represents a fulfilling material life and love for this planet. On this screen you can place anything you need to for your material life knowing that all you need will be supplied. When you need money see it piling up on the screen. Place as much of it as you need on the screen. PAUSE.

Now mentally repeat after me: this money represents all the money I need for myself, my family and friends. I always have as much money as I need. I trust the Universe to give me all the money that I need. I enjoy the way I make money and I am never greedy. I will use money to help support me and my fellow man. Money is payment for energy I have given. I work with the Universal Law of give and take. The more I give the more I get. I am at peace with myself. I always see enough money around me. PAUSE.

Now go forward in time say a year. PAUSE. See yourself the way you want to be financially. PAUSE. Bring this image to the present and place it on the screen.
Now mentally repeat after me: I know I am a keeper of planet Earth and I never take from the earth that which I cannot put back. I love my home and I take great care of it. This is an abundant Universe. There is enough for all. PAUSE.

I am aware of my physical body and I take great care of it. I exercise it and nourish it well. I take care of myself. I take care of my fellow man. PAUSE.

Now see yourself walking in the country on the green grass - every step you take you are loving the earth. See yourself with a friend and sharing this moment with them. See yourself in a red and gold light representing your financial and spiritual wealth. PAUSE.

Picture a friend by your side. PAUSE. See this red and gold light around your friend. See everyone with this red and gold light energy around them having enough financial and spiritual wealth to share with all and every one of us. Believe this is possible. Believe it now. PAUSE.
Say to yourself "I am rich in wealth and spirit always" and repeat this until I talk again. PAUSE for 30 seconds.

Now press the button and return the screen to its place. PAUSE You have now balanced your base chakra. Now it is time to return to the temple and consciousness. PAUSE. Count yourself out in the usual manner, from 10 to 1 as you climb the staircase, and then 5 to 1 to open your eyes.

Sit in meditation and concentrate on your abdomen chakra front and back, breath in the colour orange at the abdomen and chant Ooh resonating with the abdomen chakra for five minutes.

ABDOMEN CHAKRA

Go to your room of enlightenment using the 1-2-3 countdown, followed by the descending staircase while slowly counting 1-10 on each step. I will stop talking while you do this. PAUSE for 1 minute. You are now in your room of enlightenment.

When we enter our room we are here to heal ourselves as well as others. We are here to gather knowledge and information according to our need. We are here to benefit the planet and mankind. We wish no harm to any other person or living thing on this planet or on any other. When we enter our room of enlightenment we replenish our soul and heal our body and mind. We are here to learn and reconnect to higher wisdom to bring this into our conscious daily living. We are here to strengthen our weaknesses and recognise our strengths. We are here to love ourselves as well as others. PAUSE. When I suggest these words please mentally repeat them after me:
I agree to use these methods at this level for the good of all humanity. I can cleanse the abdomen chakra with the colour orange and the sound Ooh. When I do this I will not develop any illnesses associated with the abdomen chakra such as lower back trouble, impotence, frigidity or bladder problems. I will always maintain a perfectly healthy body and mind. Now, settle into a comfortable position in your chair. PAUSE. Press your control button and allow your screen to descend in front of you. See that screen turn a bright orange. PAUSE. This screen represents a balanced emotional life. On this screen you can place anything you need to help balance your emotions. PAUSE.
Picture yourself in a garden. PAUSE. See the lawn, the

trees, the bushes, hear the birds singing. PAUSE. Now if you look around the flower beds, here and there are weeds growing between the new buds. These undesirable weeds symbolise all the fears and frustrations, all the humiliations, all the negative happenings in your life. They also represent all the negative conditionings such as feelings of inferiority, and of inadequacy. They represent all refusals, all disappointments, all negative statements about yourself that anyone might have made in your life. These weeds also symbolise all the anger you have felt towards other people in the past and maybe are still feeling right now.

Now find some gardening gloves and a trowel. They are there for you somewhere in your garden. PAUSE. Now dig up all the weeds and put them in one big pile. As you pick each one you can put names on them to represent negative events in your life - some of them might represent subconscious wishes for failure, or dislike for some particular person, or some of them may represent laziness or spite someone holds against you. Some may represent fears from the past. PAUSE. Whatever those weeds symbolise gather them altogether now into one heap. Then I want you to set fire to those weeds - whatever the weeds might symbolise they have to be burnt out of your garden. PAUSE.

Now look around your garden and check there are no more weeds left. Pick any unwanted weeds that are left and place them on the rest of the pile. Once you have seen them burnt completely allow the ashes to blow away in the wind. PAUSE.

Now look around your garden and choose a tree you like. PAUSE. Now walk towards it and touch it - feel the barks texture and see what it looks like - if it doesn't feel or look good help it. PAUSE. Now look into its roots - see them and if they need nurturing help them. PAUSE. Now climb the tree to its branches. PAUSE. If they need to be more healthy help them in any way you choose. PAUSE. Now stand at the top of the tree and fly. Fly higher and higher. PAUSE for 10 seconds. Now fly back to the garden to the tree. PAUSE. Become the tree. How does that feel? PAUSE. .The tree is you and represents how you feel in your life in the present. PAUSE. Now stand in the garden again. See how tidy and clean you have made it. You can already see the flowers opening their buds. You can see the trees begin to blossom. Then feel that new growth taking place in yourself. You are opening up like a flower to the sun. Your emotions are cleansed and you can grow. All is well in your garden. PAUSE.

Now say to yourself "All is well in my Universe" and repeat this until I talk again. PAUSE for 30 seconds.

Now press the button and return the screen to its place. PAUSE. You have now balanced your abdomen chakra. Now it is time to return to the temple and consciousness. PAUSE. Count yourself out in the usual manner, from 10 to 1 as you climb the staircase, and then 5 to 1 to open your eyes.

༺༻༺༻༺༻

༺Before you enter the next visualisation, you need a pen and paper. You then draw a large cross. In each empty corner you place a personal goal and be as specific as possible such as "I want to be promoted to Manager (name the place you work)".

You can write or draw it or glue a picture of your goal. You need four goals for this exercise. You can use any affirmations you have chosen from the affirmation exercise or, other suggestions are: "I want to be a good clairvoyant and healer"; "I want to become a successful, skilled (name the goal)"; "I want to release all feelings of inferiority"; "I want to help other people in my work"; "I am confident"; "I never give up until I have achieved my goal"; "I never lose faith in myself and my own power"; "It is alright to make mistakes" and so on.

Now study each corner and absorb each goal through words or picture. Now keep that picture near your shrine or in a special place. You can look back in six months and see if you have achieved your goals. You have to picture your goals as in the next visualisation for the next month every day for it to be truly effective. Repeat these goals in your mind every day even if you cannot do this visualisation every day. You may find your goals will change and that is fine. Life is forever changing and much of what manifests in your life is what you need and not always what you want. You receive what you need, to learn your lessons. Never forget you have chosen these lessons and have created much of your environment through your own thinking. You are master of your destiny and by placing all your goals in your subconscious you are sure to achieve all you ask for in the best possible manner. Some goals are not achieved for two or three years but undoubtedly opportunities arise through asking the Universe to help you. If you work with the Universe you will receive all that you need and more.

₰

Sit in meditation and concentrate on your solar plexus chakra front and back, breath in the colour yellow at the solar plexus and chant Ah resonating with the solar plexus chakra for five minutes.

✒ SOLAR PLEXUS CHAKRA

Go to your room of enlightenment using the 1-2-3 countdown, followed by the descending staircase while slowly counting 1-10 on each step. I will stop talking while you do this. PAUSE for 1 minute. You are now in your room of enlightenment.

When we enter our room we are here to heal ourselves as well as others. We are here to gather knowledge and information according to our need. We are here to benefit the planet and mankind. We wish no harm to any other person or living thing on this planet or on any other. When we enter our room of enlightenment we replenish our soul and heal our body and mind. We are here to learn and reconnect to higher wisdom to bring this into our conscious daily living. We are here to strengthen our weaknesses and recognise our strengths. We are here to love ourselves as well as others. PAUSE. When I suggest these words please mentally repeat them after me:
I agree to use these methods at this level for the good of all humanity. I can cleanse the solar plexus chakra with the colour yellow and the sound Ah. When I do this I will not develop any illnesses associated with the solar plexus chakra such as ulcers, diabetes, hypoglycaemia or muscular disorders. I will always maintain a perfectly healthy body and mind.

Now, settle into a comfortable position in your chair. PAUSE. Press your control button and allow your screen to descend in front of you. See that screen turn a bright yellow. PAUSE.

This screen represents self-fulfillment and achievement. On this screen you can place anything you need to help you achieve your aims and goals. PAUSE.

Now get a felt tip pen and draw on your screen a large cross. PAUSE. Now fill in your four goals by writing the words, drawing or visualising the picture in each corner. PAUSE for 2 minutes. Now write under the cross "With harm to no-one" and sign your name. PAUSE for 10 seconds.

Now mentally repeat after me: "I now absorb all my goals and send them to my higher self". PAUSE. Your goals are now imprinted in your subconscious mind and will materialise in the physical world in the manner and time that is relevant on your path. You will manifest all things when your soul is deemed ready.

Now I want you to have a picture of yourself, the way you want yourself to be. See yourself looking calm and relaxed, see yourself looking confident, see yourself looking totally in control and achieving all your aims. Now take some time now to allow your subconscious mind to absorb this picture, and these suggestions, so that it can then feed them back into your daily living, so that you can be the person you choose to be.

Now press the button and return the screen to its place. PAUSE. You have now balanced your solar plexus chakra. Now it is time to return to the temple and consciousness. PAUSE. Count yourself out in the usual manner, from 10 to 1 as you climb the staircase, and then 5 to 1 to open your eyes.

Sit in meditation and concentrate on your heart chakra front and back, breathe in the colour emerald green and then pink at the centre of the heart chakra and chant Ay resonating with the heart area for five minutes.

ᔆHEART CHAKRA

Go to your room of enlightenment using the 1-2-3 countdown, followed by the descending staircase while slowly counting 1-10 on each step. I will stop talking while you do this. PAUSE for 1 minute. You are now in your room of enlightenment.

When we enter our room we are here to heal ourselves as well as others. We are here to gather knowledge and information according to our need. We are here to benefit the planet and mankind. We wish no harm to any other person or living thing on this planet or on any other. When we enter our room of enlightenment we replenish our soul and heal our body and mind. We are here to learn and reconnect to higher wisdom to bring this into our conscious daily living. We are here to strengthen our weaknesses and recognise our strengths. We are here to love ourselves as well as others. PAUSE. When I suggest these words please mentally repeat them after me:
I agree to use these methods at this level for the good of all humanity. I can cleanse the heart chakra with the colour green and the sound Ay. When I do this I will not develop any illnesses associated with the heart chakra such as high blood pressure, heart disease, lung disease, asthma or any other lung or heart disorders. I will always maintain a perfectly healthy body and mind.

Now, settle into a comfortable position in your chair. PAUSE. Press your control button and allow your screen to descend in front of you. See that screen turn a bright green. PAUSE. Then see it turn pink which represents unconditional love. PAUSE. Now get a pen and write UNCONDITIONAL LOVE on your screen. PAUSE. Now think about what these words mean to you while visualising UNCONDITIONAL LOVE. If your thoughts or visualisation start to drift away, bring your mind back to the words UNCONDITIONAL LOVE. PAUSE. Use these words to focus and discipline your mind whilst absorbing the power of Love. PAUSE. The power of love for yourself and for others. I am going to pause for two minutes as you focus on unconditional love and the pink screen. PAUSE for 2 minutes.

Now mentally repeat after me: When I give love without wanting anything in return I find a peace I never imagined. I become closer to my higher self and soul level. I become close to Universal Love and God. When I become closer to God in these peaceful moments I start to touch upon blissfulness. I start to smile within and my smile spreads over all the souls I meet and over the whole Universe. My every look reflects my joyous soul. I stop believing that I have to go through mental ups and downs. No matter what happens, I remember I am made in the true image of Spirit. The living joy in all things and the Fountain of Cosmic Bliss which showers me with its spray and sends joy trickling through my thoughts, my every cell and tissue of my whole being. I am in tune with my soul and my creator. PAUSE.

I remember at night in the state of deep dreaming sleep,

which is unconscious soul-perception, I am happy all the while. So during the day, regardless of how much I am disturbed by difficult mental trials and upheavals, I must keep trying all the time to be inwardly ever newly joyous. I aim to live in a blissful state in touch with my soul. I intend to shine light and love to all I meet. I intend to have Heaven on Earth. I intend only to work with light and love and draw in spirit beings of light and love to me. In these aware moments I call an angel and I feel an angel around me. I feel and see this angel or many angels in my room of enlightenment. PAUSE for 1 minute.

I know I am never alone and that all my prayers are heard. I send a prayer for some people I know who need healing now. PAUSE for 1 minute.

Now feel your heart chakra open to receive Love and Light more than it has ever opened before. PAUSE. Now mentally repeat after me for 1 minute "I open my heart to love, compassion and empathy". PAUSE for 1 minute.

Now press the button and return the screen to its place. PAUSE. You have now balanced your heart chakra. Now it is time to return to the temple and consciousness. PAUSE. Count yourself out in the usual manner, from 10 to 1 as you climb the staircase, and then 5 to 1 to open your eyes.

ଙ✶ଙ✶ଙ✶

Sit in meditation and concentrate on your throat chakra front and back, breath in the colour turquoise at the throat and chant Eee resonating with the throat chakra for five minutes.

THROAT CHAKRA

Go to your room of enlightenment using the 1-2-3 countdown, followed by the descending staircase while slowly counting 1-10 on each step. I will stop talking while you do this. PAUSE for 1 minute. You are now in your room of enlightenment.

When we enter our room we are here to heal ourselves as well as others. We are here to gather knowledge and information according to our need. We are here to benefit the planet and mankind. We wish no harm to any other person or living thing on this planet or on any other. When we enter our room of enlightenment we replenish our soul and heal our body and mind. We are here to learn and reconnect to higher wisdom to bring this into our conscious daily living. We are here to strengthen our weaknesses and recognise our strengths. We are here to love ourselves as well as others. PAUSE. When I suggest these words please mentally repeat them after me:
I agree to use these methods at this level for the good of all humanity. I can cleanse the throat chakra with the colour turquoise and the sound Eee. When I do this I will not develop any illnesses associated with the throat chakra such as colds, thyroid problems, hearing problems, stiff neck, laryngitis or throat problems. I will always maintain a perfectly healthy body and mind.

Now, settle into a comfortable position in your chair. PAUSE. Press your control button and allow your screen to descend in front of you. See that screen turn a bright turquoise. PAUSE.

This screen will help you communicate with your guide. Your guide can be male or female and is there to advise you about any mental, emotional or physical problems that arise for you or another. He or she will advise you about anything such as career, moving home or relationship problems. Use your guide freely. Your guide is an excellent channel of intelligence in touch with Universal Love and Wisdom.

Now mentally say "I welcome my guide. Please appear on my screen" and see your guide appear on the screen. Thank your guide for appearing. PAUSE. Your guide will be here every time you enter your room of enlightenment. Now stay as long as you wish to talk with your guide. You may hear your answers or see them written on the screen. Ask your guide if he or she has a name. Find out all you need to know. PAUSE for one minute. Now say thank you to your guide and mentally say "I love you, I bless you and release you to my higher self".

Your guide can now talk to you at any time even in conscious beta state. You will always be aware of receiving guidance from now on. PAUSE.

And now go into the silence. PAUSE for one minute. Go back in time. Go back hundreds of years. Go back thousands of years. Go back to the beginning of time. PAUSE. Still in the silence and darkness, you hear a beautiful sound becoming louder and louder and with that sound comes a small light becoming brighter and brighter. PAUSE. The sound allows the light to form patterns. Watch the many patterns forming from the sound. PAUSE. Watch the many colours wafting through the beautiful shapes and patterns. PAUSE. Then the sound slowly turns to a word. Hear that word. PAUSE. These sounds, colours and word represent your resonance and frequency at this moment of time. PAUSE. Now listen to these words and let them echo through your mind. "In the beginning was the Word, and the Word was with God and the Word was God". PAUSE for 30 seconds.

Now press the button and return the screen to its place. PAUSE You have now balanced your throat chakra. Now it is time to return to the temple and consciousness. PAUSE. Count yourself out in the usual manner, from 10 to 1 as you climb the staircase, and then 5 to 1 to open your eyes.

❧❧❧

Sit in meditation and concentrate on your third eye front and back of head, breath in the colour indigo at the third and chant Om resonating with the third eye for five minutes.

❧THIRD EYE

Go to your room of enlightenment using the 1-2-3 count-down, followed by the descending staircase while slowly counting 1-10 on each step. I will stop talking while you do this. PAUSE for 1 minute. You are now in your room of enlightenment.

When we enter our room we are here to heal ourselves as well as others. We are here to gather knowledge and information according to our need. We are here to benefit the planet and mankind. We wish no harm to any other person or living thing on this planet or on any other. When we enter our room of enlightenment we replenish our soul and heal our body and mind. We are here to learn and reconnect to higher wisdom to bring this into our conscious daily living. We are here to strengthen our weaknesses and recognise our strengths. We are here to love ourselves as well as others. PAUSE. When I suggest these words please mentally repeat them after me: I agree to use these methods at this level for the good of all humanity. I can cleanse the third eye with the colour indigo and the sound Om. When I do this I will not develop any malfunctions associated with the third eye such as blindness, headaches, nightmares, eyestrain, and blurred vision. I will always maintain a perfectly healthy body and mind.

Now, settle into a comfortable position in your chair. PAUSE. Press your control button and allow your screen to descend in front of you. See that screen turn to indigo. PAUSE.

In a few moments you are going to scan your body externally and internally with your minds eye. You will have the chance to correct any abnormalities if you should find them. This will in turn help you treat another person and expand your X ray vision. PAUSE. Now imagine a beam of light pouring through your pineal gland into your third eye. You can send this beam of light anywhere in the body to see any organ or part you choose. This is your X ray vision. PAUSE.

When I tap my hands, project your body onto the screen so you can examine it. TAP HANDS - PAUSE.

See your body standing in front of you now. PAUSE. Have

your body face you and remove any clothing if it has any on. PAUSE.

Start scanning the skin of your body with your beam of light from your third eye, starting at your head and moving down to your toes. Pay particular attention to skin tone, scars, swelling, lumps, burns, extra flab and bruises. If you notice any imbalance correct it. If you see flab you wish to get rid of, see it slimming down... You have a minute to scan and repair, if necessary, the front of your body skin. PAUSE for one minute.

Now when I tap my hands, have your body turn around so you can examine the rear skin. TAP HANDS - PAUSE. You are now observing your body's rear exterior. PAUSE. In a moment, when I tap my hands, begin scanning your back skin from head to foot just as you did for the front skin. Correct any imbalance if you see any. You have one minute to do this. TAP HANDS - PAUSE.

Now when I tap my hands have your body walk away from you for five steps and stop. Observe the walk and correct the stance if necessary. TAP HANDS - PAUSE. Now when I tap my hands have your body turn around and walk five steps back toward you and stop. Observe the walk and correct the stance if necessary. TAP HANDS - PAUSE.

When I tap my hands, project your X ray vision into your skeletal structure in the skull. TAP HANDS - PAUSE. Now slowly scan all your bones from head to toe. If you notice any abnormality, correct it. Pay attention to the joints for spurs or excess calcification build-up. Sand the joints smooth and lubricate them. Put your skeletal structure into excellent condition. Be thorough and precise. PAUSE. for two minutes. Now when I tap my hands, project your X ray vision into your head. TAP HANDS - PAUSE.

Examine everything in your head - your teeth, eyes, brain, ears, cells, nerves, blood flow, glands. Notice colours, movements. If you detect any abnormality, correct it. Be as thorough as you can. You have two minutes. PAUSE for two minutes. Now project into your chest and body trunk. TAP HANDS - PAUSE. Examine your heart, lungs, liver, stomach, bladder, kidneys, pancreas, sex glands. Notice colour, movement, nerves, cells, and blood flow. If you see any abnormality, correct it. Be thorough. You have three minutes - PAUSE for three minutes.

Now when I tap my hands, begin exploring anything you have not yet looked at. Your throat, arms, hands, legs, feet, lymphatic system, nervous system. If you see any abnormality correct it. PAUSE for 2 minutes.

In a few moments I am going to ask you to perform an unusual and extremely beneficial exercise. I am going to ask you to physically reach out with both hands and lift the head off your body in front of you and to bring it back and place it over your head where you are sitting. This is not harmful in any way because you are superimposing an energy configuration over another energy configuration. The actual physical body is not affected.

In the future you will experience doing this with other people's heads. That is, you will place their head onto yours. This allows you to sense their emotions, thought processes, fears, personality, character and so on. This an excellent tool and for now you are practising with your own head - so you may not experience anything you are not already aware of. PAUSE.

Now when I tap my hands, physically reach out with your hands and lift the head from your body in front of you and bring it back and place it onto your head. TAP HANDS - PAUSE. Experience the feeling of the superimposed head. Sense the emotions... the thoughts... ask any questions of yourself that you wish. PAUSE for 10 seconds. In the future you can use this technique to explore the emotions, thoughts, fears, character, and personality of other people. PAUSE. Now when I tap my hands physically reach up and remove the superimposed head and return it to the body in front of you. TAP HANDS - PAUSE.

You now place yourself in a pink bubble of love and protection, clear the screen knowing you are fully healthy. You have now explored your own body.

Now its time to explore someone else who you know needs healing. Invite this person into your room of enlightenment. Put this person on your screen. Now go through this whole process again, scan their skin front and back, see them walk back and forward, and then move onto the head, chest, trunk and rest of the body as before. Then put their head on yours and ask questions to see if there are any blocks and ask questions to understand their mental condition, and ask their higher self to guide them through any negativity, send them thoughts of love and well being, . You have 5 minutes to investigate. PAUSE for 5 minutes.

Now place them in a pink bubble of love and protection and say "I thank you for coming, I love you and may Gods will be done"

Now press the button and return the screen to its place. PAUSE You have now balanced your third eye chakra. Now it is time to return to the temple and consciousness. PAUSE. Count yourself out in the usual manner, from 10 to 1 as you climb the staircase, and then 5 to 1 to open your eyes.

Sit in meditation and concentrate on the crown of your head, breath in the colour violet at the crown and chant a high pitched NgNgNg like a bell resonating with the crown for five minutes.

CROWN CHAKRA

Go to your room of enlightenment using the 1-2-3 count-down, followed by the descending staircase while slowly counting 1-10 on each step. I will stop talking while you do this. PAUSE for 1 minute. You are now in your room of enlightenment.

When we enter our room we are here to heal ourselves as well as others. We are here to gather knowledge and information according to our need. We are here to benefit the planet and mankind. We wish no harm to any other person or living thing on this planet or on any other. When we enter our room of enlightenment we replenish our soul and heal our body and mind. We are here to learn and reconnect to higher wisdom to bring this into our conscious daily living. We are here to strengthen our

weaknesses and recognise our strengths. We are here to love ourselves as well as others. PAUSE.
When I suggest these words please mentally repeat them after me:
I agree to use these methods at this level for the good of all humanity. I can cleanse the crown with the colour violet and the sound Ngngng. When I do this I will not develop any malfunctions associated with the crown such as depression, alienation, confusion and boredom. I will always maintain a perfectly healthy body and mind.

Now, settle into a comfortable position in your chair. PAUSE. Press your control button and allow your screen to descend in front of you. See that screen turn to violet. PAUSE.

You now think of the man Jesus on his path to being The Christ, just before his full awakening. PAUSE. The first person or thing you see you go towards and help it. It does not matter what this person is doing or thing is, just help it. PAUSE for 10 seconds.

Take a note of how it has changed and how this can help your path to enlightenment. PAUSE.

You now see a beam of white light that forms a tunnel of light at the top of your head. PAUSE. You can travel through this tunnel of light to anywhere in the Universe. You can travel to a different planet, galaxy, visit different cosmic beings. You can travel back to the past, to Ancient Egypt, Lemuria, Atlantis if you wish. You can travel back or forward in time. You now have that choice. So choose a place. PAUSE. Now travel upward higher and higher

*through your tunnel of light to your destination.
Investigate and return to your body in 5 minutes.
PAUSE.*

*Now repeat this mentally after me:
I allow myself to be a clear channel for divine healing and offer to help others in any way possible through my psychic abilities. I ask that Universal Knowledge is filtered into my conscious mind so that it can be of benefit to mankind and if I am to be in service, I ask to always be shown the way.*

Now press the button and return the screen to its place. PAUSE. You have now balanced your crown chakra. Now it is time to return to the temple and consciousness. PAUSE. Count yourself out in the usual manner, from 10 to 1 as you climb the staircase, and then 5 to 1 to open your eyes.

♡MORE VISUALISATIONS
♡HEAL YOUR LIFE

Write or remember in detail all good and bad events in your life, then list all that you have accomplished and learnt. You may begin to see a pattern occurring or perhaps the same circumstance with different people. Or maybe something happened in the past that is now blocking your path or you are too attached to certain people. You may feel let down by high expectations of others, and so on.

Use the following visualisations in your room of enlightenment to heal your life. Make sure you have no interruptions from people or the telephone. Please remember to put a bubble of Light and Love around you for added protection and feel your feet firmly rooted to the ground when you finish each visualisation.

....

....

....

....

....

....

⌘VISUALISATION TO CLEANSE YOUR LIFE

Go to your room of enlightenment as usual. Close your eyes and take some very deep breaths into your body. Breathe into your feet and relax them.

Breathe into your legs and relax them. Breathe into your hips and relax them. Breathe into your abdomen and relax it. Breathe into your chest and relax it. Breathe into your back and relax it. Breathe into your neck and shoulders and relax them. Breathe into your face and relax it. Breathe into your scalp and relax it.

Start to go back in time throughout your life back to just before entering your mothers womb. You imagine a black rope attached to your body and allow this rope to grow longer attached to your body as you slowly grow in the womb and in daily life. This rope represents every word and event that has effected you negatively. For each event that you remember you tie a knot in the rope. You do this as slowly as you wish.
When you have reached the present moment you cut the rope from your body and throw it away. You throw it away somewhere that you can burn it or completely lose it in some way. You see it disappear and disintegrate.

You can do this exercise as many times as you wish until the rope disappears completely.

Remember to put a bubble of Light and Love around you with no holes in the bubble. Feel roots from your feet holding you to the Earth. Call yourself back in the normal manner from your room of enlightenment.

✑CLEANSING RELATIONSHIPS

Think of a relationship you need to heal and the person concerned.

Close your eyes, find your room of enlightenment and relax your body as above. Imagine yourself walking along a beach. Feel the air against your skin, the sand beneath your feet, hear the waves of the sea and the sounds of Nature around you. Then find a spot on the sand and draw a figure of eight. You stand in one circle and see the other person in the other circle.

You say what you need to say first. For the reply you become the other person and listen to the reply. You become you again and say something else and become the other person and listen to the reply. You do this until the issue is resolved as much as possible.

You then ask your higher self what it is you are learning from this person and situation. You then ask the other person's higher self what they are learning from you and the situation.

You then put them in a pink bubble of love and send them love sincerely.

You then place yourself in a pink bubble of love and protection to end the session. Come out of your room of enlightenment in the same way. Make sure you are grounded by roots holding your feet to the Earth and you can rub your hands to come back into the room.

HEALING THE RELATIONSHIP WITH YOUR PARENTS

Go to your room of enlightenment and relax as before. Go to a beautiful garden where there are wonderful flowers, plants and trees. Picture yourself breathing in the pure fresh air.

See yourself at five years old playing. Give yourself a big hug and lots of love. Feel how vulnerable and innocent you are. Accept yourself for who you are. Place that picture of yourself in your heart.

Now see your mother as a five year old. Give her a big hug and lots of love. Accept her feelings and her vulnerability. Love her for who she is and place her in your heart.

Now see your father as an innocent five year old. Give him a big hug and tons of love. See him playing and accept him for who he is. Place this happy picture in your heart. Fill your heart full of unconditional love for you and your parents. Imagine a rose quartz crystal in your heart lovingly energising your relationship to your self and your parents.

Come out of your room of enlightenment as usual. Slowly find yourself back in the room making sure you are grounded with roots holding you to the Earth and a bubble of white light around you for protection.

You can do this exercise as many times as you like to heal any wounds or past grievances.

⁊OPENING YOUR AWARENESS

These exercises will help your psychic abilities and awareness immensely.

⁊Pick three objects of different materials you want to work on such as glass, wood, fabric or metal. Study these objects closely and feel their texture.
Go to your room of enlightenment in the usual way. Now visualise the first object and place it in front of you. Examine the object externally with your X ray vision. What colour is it? Is it rough or smooth? Is it cold or hot? And then go inside it and under the surface of it. Is the molecular structure dense or roomy? Is it light or dark? What colour is it? Is it cold or hot? Then go to the centre. How different is it to the external?
Do this with all the objects. You are learning to project your X ray vision to any point at which you want to focus. Come out of your room of enlightenment in the usual way.

⁊Now choose a plant or flower you like. Examine it in every way, smell it and feel its texture.
Enter your room of enlightenment in the usual way. Visualise the plant or flower you have chosen. Examine it externally. Notice the leaf or petal shape and thickness and then go inside the leaf or petal. Again check it for molecular structure, light and colour, and temperature. Also what can you hear. Is it different to the inanimate objects? Is there movement? Check out the stem internally. And then the roots.
Enjoy the experience and see what you are learning. Come out of your room of enlightenment in the normal way.

HEALING ANIMALS

Now choose an animal, go to your room of enlightenment and visualise it in much the same way as we looked at the human body. Check all the systems and organs of the body as well as externally. Change any abnormalities by adding colour or removing growths or lumps. You now have wonderful tools to play with and use for the benefit of all.

CALLING A PERSON IN SPIRIT

Along your path you are likely to feel spirit around you and have an awareness of being visited. Now you can talk to them much more easily in your room of enlightenment.

Go to your room of enlightenment in the usual way. Pull down the turquoise screen and ask that your guide appear. Your guide is the door-keeper to allow anyone else in from the spirit world. Ask if anyone wants to speak with you or you can help spirit in any way and see what happens. A spirit could be lost and you need to ask your guide to take them to the light. Have a conversation with spirit if appropriate.

When finished say to your spirit and guide "God bless you and please return to the Light". Put yourself in white light with mirrors around you if you wish and return in the usual way to conscious awareness.

ASTRAL TRAVELLING

You can travel anywhere in your mind to visit a friend, do absent healing or visit another part of the world.

Go to your room of enlightenment in the usual way. Pull down your indigo screen to open your third eye. To practice imagine you are now coming out of your body and out of the top of your home. You are moving above your street. Notice the cars, houses, colours of paint work, the road and pavement and the people. Take some time before you move further afield to any destination you wish to investigate. As you travel always send love to the planet and the people you meet.

Take as long as you want before you find yourself above your home and re-entering your body. Come back slowly into your body. Do not worry you are always attached by a silver cord. You will never leave it permanently. You can always ask your guide and angel to be with you on your travels.

When you are ready leave your room of enlightenment in the usual way.

CHAKRAS

The Universe is composed of spinning wheels of energy. At the root of all Nature, the wheel is the circle of life through all aspects of existence.

At the inner core of our being are spinning wheels of energy connected to different parts of our body and mainly to our spine. These energy centres are called chakras. Chakra is a Sanskrit word meaning wheel or disc. They are seen clairvoyantly as wheel-like spinning vortexes. There are seven main ones attached to the spine of our body. They are seen spinning front and back of our body. They have been called lotuses as they resemble petals of flowers and associated to the sacred flower in India. From bottom to top there are seen 4, 6, 10, 12, 16, 2, 1000 petals.

The chakras or lotuses, are seven basic energy centres within our subtle body or aura. The aura is a reflection of our body, thoughts and feelings and can be measured as an electromagnetic force field. All living beings and plant-life have this force field or aura and this has been photographed by Kirlian photography. We need to learn to cleanse our aura and chakras to be healthy in body, mind and spirit.

The seven main chakras correspond to nerve ganglia where there is a high degree of nervous activity and to glands in the endocrine system. The chakras reflect the health of the body.

They form the connecting channel between mind and body and can be measured as patterns of electromagnetic activity, centred around the major nerve ganglia. They can be used to diagnose and heal illnesses, and have corresponding associations in the physical world. We have departed from the classical Indian interpretation of chakras which goes back to before 2000 BC, and started to use them in a modern day understanding. Classic interpretation advised repression of the lower chakras dealing with earthly matters to achieve higher states. We now tend to use all our chakras and keep them in balance when we learn methods of cleansing them.

As we ascend and heighten our vibration we are to use many more, the additional ones being the omega chakra, 8 inches below the spine, connecting us to the planetary consciousness, and the alpha, 8 inches above your head, connecting you to your fifth dimensional Lightbody. There are then more above the head connecting you to your group soul level, the Christed level of spirit-self, the I AM Presence and the Source. (See An Ascension Handbook by Tony Stubbs, Published by Oughten House ISBN 1-880666-08-1)

There are many associations to the seven main chakras and below are the main ones used in The Call of an Angel Course. You can use these associations to cleanse each chakra by meditating on the colour for each one as you close your eyes and sense them one by one spinning at the back and front of your body. The colours are based on a psychological background to the chakras and not the colours always seen clairvoyantly or in the ancient belief system.

You can do the same with the sound pitching the note for each one, uniting with planetary energy and affirmations. There are movements and many other associations not mentioned.

Alone or in a group situation this can be a very strong experience and at first it may be a better idea to have a recognised teacher to talk you through these methods of opening the chakras. Please open them with caution. It will be excellent if you simply cleanse them with colour, sound and movement.

If you do open the chakras in deep meditation in your own home alone, ask for that bubble of light for protection and be sure that you close down each chakra like a flower closing its petals - at first you need these safety guards. As you get used to opening the chakras and the heightened vibrations you will feel more and more safe in this process. You can outgrow this process eventually. At first you can be a little over excited and too high on the whole experience. Take one step at a time and be patient. Don't expect spirit visitations all the time or amazing things to happen every day. It doesn't work like that. The best way is slow and easy. Remember you are working with Nature. KEEP YOUR FEET ON THE GROUND AND KEEP WATCHING YOUR EGO.

ASSOCIATIONS TO SEVEN MAIN CHAKRAS

The chakras spin back and front of body seen 6" in diameter and about 1" from the body.

ONE - BASE OF SPINE

KEYWORDS:	matter, survival, grounding, the body, food, beginning, unity, individuality, earth
PLANET:	Saturn, Earth
SOUND:	O (rope)
COLOUR:	red
AFFIRMATIONS:	I am safe and secure at all times
	Life is good
	I have a strong foundation in life

TWO - ABDOMEN

KEYWORDS:	change, polarities (male and female), movement, pleasure, emotions, sensuality, nurturance, clairsentience (sensing others), socialisation, water
PLANET:	Pluto, Moon
SOUND:	OO (due)
COLOUR:	orange
AFFIRMATIONS:	I feel the joy and freedom
	I feel all is well in my Universe
	I feel pleasure in all that I do

THREE - SOLAR PLEXUS

KEYWORDS:	fire, power, will, energy, metabolism, technology (harnessing power), transformation, magic, humour
PLANET:	Sun, Mars
SOUND:	ah (father)
COLOUR:	yellow
AFFIRMATIONS:	I am worthy
	I am worth my weight in gold
	I laugh and all is forgotten and healed

FOUR - HEART

KEYWORDS:	love, air, breath, balance, relationship, affinity, unity, healing, empathy
PLANET:	Venus, Neptune
SOUND:	Ay (play)
COLOUR:	Green, Pink
AFFIRMATIONS:	I open my heart to love
	The more love I receive, the more love I give sincerely
	Love is the purpose of my life

FIVE - THROAT

KEYWORDS:	ether, vibration, communication, mantras, creativity, telepathy, media
PLANET:	Mercury
SOUND:	Ee (seed)
COLOUR:	Turquoise
AFFIRMATIONS:	I allow the expression of my true self to find form
	I express myself creatively and openly
	I express the best of who I am now

SIX - THIRD EYE

KEYWORDS:	light, colour, seeing, visualisation, imagination, clairvoyance, hologram (reflected record)
PLANET:	Neptune, Jupiter
SOUND:	Om
COLOUR:	Indigo
AFFIRMATIONS:	I open myself to my intuition and deepest knowing
	I radiate love, clarity and integrity
	My thoughts are clear and focused

SEVEN - CROWN

KEYWORDS:	thought, knowing, information, understanding, transcendence, meditation, enlightenment, consciousness
PLANET:	Chiron, Sirius, Uranus, Pluto
SOUND:	NgNgNg
COLOUR:	Violet
AFFIRMATIONS:	I am at one with the Universe
	I am at peace
	Love and Light surrounds me, protects and nourishes me

SOUND

"I will sing with the Spirit, and I will sing with the understanding also" 1 Cor. 14:15

BRIEF HISTORY

Since the dawn of civilisation music has been used to influence men's minds and spirits and thus their bodies. The Chinese, Hindus, Egyptians, Babylonians, Greeks and Arabs all used music to soothe and heal. We are told that more than one thousand years before the birth of Christ, "David took a harp and played with his hand, so Saul was refreshed and was well, and the evil spirit departed from him" (I Samuel 16.23). The Jews were said to be musicians of great skill and the Bible names many string, wind and percussion instruments, such as harp, lute, viol, cornet, dulcimer, organ, pipe, trumpet, bells, cymbals, and so on.

Solomon's Temple had an orchestra of wind instruments, a male choir in which each member had a minimum of five years training and a boy's choir to add to the sweetness.

The ancient Egyptians used music to cure and in 287 BC it was said by the Greek who studied their methods, that the flute music was played to sufferers from sciatica, rheumatism and other pains including the stings of insects. In the cool of the evening rulers and high officials would glide down the Nile in their barges and relax from the strains and stresses of official duties to the music of the lute and the harp.

According to Cyril Scott, the Egyptians used third tones. As a result it was less subtle than Indian, which used quarter tones, and worked closely with the mind and mentality, whereas third tones work closely with the emotions. In Western music we use half tones evoking materialism.

In Egypt, the esoteric schools were called "The Mysteries", and in one of their most important ceremonies of initiation, the candidate, with the aid of music and other rites, was put into a trance, from which he emerged with a knowledge of the afterlife. A third tone is said to loosen the emotional body from the physical and so induce "astral trance". Through this they learnt from actual experience that they were immortal.

Egyptians regarded music itself as having a divine origin, and that harmony and the various instruments had been discovered and invented by the Gods. Thus, according to them, Hermes discovered the principle of voices and sounds and invented the lyre while Osiris invented the flute.

Music seemed to be associated with nearly all activities in daily life. Whatever their work they always had songs to sing. Their song was especially suited to the particular occupation in which they were engaged.

There was even someone to beat time.

In Lemuria, way before Egypt and Atlantis, it is said the inhabitants were energy beings and knew the sounds of Nature. They sang the tunes of the animals and plants being completely in harmony with the environment.

In Ancient India, great stress was placed upon both the healing and destructive powers of music. The sounds made by humans carried an influence of mind over matter. They urged men to study words and sentences and produce the forms of speech known as mantras. (See list of mantras). As each sound produces a wave pattern we need to be sure we use the right words to resonate to our own personal frequency and especially our names. Mantras, especially the Om sound which makes beautiful patterns, keeps the mind occupied with the beauty of sound and permits the soul to be free in communion with the Source.

In India and Sri Lanka, there were men known as Mantracaras who composed a mantra to achieve a specific purpose, such as a cure for disease or for increase of intuition, ESP or psychic powers. The most powerful of mantras is the magical Aum or Om which can be sent for miles to heal people. It has been stated that in Sri Lanka there are Buddhists who can cure the bite of poisonous reptiles by repeating mantras.

Aum or Om is a Sanskrit root word or seed-sound symbolising that aspect of Godhead which creates and sustains all things: Cosmic Vibration. Aum of the Vedas became the sacred word Hum of the Tibetans; Amin of the moslems; and Amen of the Egyptians, Greeks, Romans, Jews, and Christians. The world's great religions state that all created things originate in the cosmic vibratory energy of Aum or Amen, the Word or Holy Ghost. "In the beginning was the Word, and the Word was with God, and the Word was God... All things were made by him (the word or Aum), and without him was not any thing made that was made" (John 1:1,3)

Primitive language was born from imitating sounds of nature and from vocal expressions responding to physical and vital movements innate with their own essential sound vibrations. In Sanskrit, said to be the very first language, sound has two aspects, the more audible sound and the subtler essential sound-element behind it, vibrant with the meaning natural to it. This vibrant sense-sound within is the real or fundamental sound, called the sphota. The outward audible sound, its instrument of expression, is called the external sound. Wouldn't it be wonderful to speak a language from the source of nature?

So to summarise, music and sound affects our minds and emotions. It affects us either consciously or subconsciously or both. It is capable of healing us and our aura, and making us whole.

VIBRATIONS

Every particle around us has a frequency and therefore every atom. Every cell within our body has a frequency. It also has the capability of responding to any other sound outside of the body. Every organ, in which cells of like vibration have gathered to form that organ, will respond as a group to particular sound vibrations. The various systems in the body will also respond to sound vibrations, as will various emotional, mental and spiritual states of consciousness. The human body is a bio-electrical system. The bio-electrical energy is created in varying frequencies through muscular actions and can be altered, strengthened or balanced through the use of music and sound.

I have channelled information about the day when we can heal frequencies very precisely within the body and in the aura with the aid of computers.

Dr Hans Jenny, a Swiss scientist and artist, describes some of the experiments he has carried out in a long study of rhythmic vibrations and presents some of the results in his books called Cymatics (from the Greek kyma, wave). Dr Jenny believed that these experiments gave us a new insight into the world of vibration.

Our world is permeated throughout by waves and vibrations. When we hear, waves travelling through the air impinge on our ears. When we speak we ourselves generate air waves with our larynx. When we turn on our radios and televisions, we are utilising a waveband. We talk about electric waves and waves of light. In an earthquake the whole earth vibrates and seismic waves are produced. There are whole stars which pulsate in regular rhythm.

And so our blood pulses through us in waves. We can hear the beat of the heart. And above all our muscles go into a state of vibration when we move them. When we flex the muscles of our arms and legs, they actually begin to vibrate. It is possible to hear muscle sounds.

A very important characteristic of wave and vibrational processes is that there is movement and an interplay of forces and the creation of forms and figures. Cymatics, the study of wave forms, illustrates dramatically the relationship between frequency and form. Specific materials subjected to specific vibrations assume specific forms. A given form can only be summoned forth at its corresponding frequency; form is a response to frequency.

Form is what we call "reality" but that reality is obviously conditional - for it is the structure of our organs of perception that is responsible for the ultimate picture. If our senses were differently attuned, reality would assume a very different aspect. We might perceive matter as motion if our senses were quicker; if they were slower, we would be aware of the apparent motion of the sun, and our whole world would appear to be motion. Using sand, oil of turpentine, lycopodium powder and other materials with specific vibrations Hans Jenny made wonderful forms and shapes.

Fabien Maman, a pioneer in sound and colour worked with Joel Sternheimer, a physicist who discovered that elementary particles vibrate at frequencies in accordance with musical laws. Together they achieved the transposition of the characteristic vibratory resonance of certain key molecules into their lower frequency musical equivalents. Fabien contends that this process has enormously important therapeutic implications in that it can be used both to stimulate healthy human cells and to harmonise and heal sick ones. He also emphasises the adverse effects of environmental noise, which should be significantly reduced if the human organism is to reach its potential of vitality and wellbeing.

He discovered that by playing a chromatic scale with tuning forks next to cancer cells, their intercellular components started to lose definition as the scale ascended and generally disintegrated between A (440 hertz) and B. Colours can appear in healthy cells. Some cancer cells explode after twenty-one minutes.

Individual cells have 'personal' qualities related to the overall condition of the person from whom they are taken. This partly accounts for the fact that when sound therapy is used therapeutically, a cure is only sometimes achieved. Disease is a disturbance in an individuals electromagnetic field and is partly programmed at birth, not only through genetic inheritance but soul inheritance or karma.

As we develop, our subtle energy fields become polluted through toxins, stress, environmental dissonance and many other factors - but babies are born free from their direct effects. It is therefore the subtle energy 'blueprint' with which we are born that largely determines our future states of wellbeing or ill-health.

THE HEALING VOICE

Toning and chanting heal mind, body and spirit. To tone with the voice every day will help you come back to wholeness. Groaning first is an excellent release of all stress and negative thoughts. (See Toning by Laurel Elizabeth Keyes (DeVorss))

Find your quiet, uninterrupted space. Place feet apart, close your eyes and shake your body and groan from the feet upwards, through your body to the top of head. As soon as the groans are over a tone is formed. Then as the tone forms hold your hands on your back at the kidneys. You rejuvenate the whole of your body in this process as according to Chinese belief the Chi, the Life Force, is held in the kidneys and thus by holding them you are rebuilding the Chi in your body. Keep toning and sounding your note until your hands are ready to be unglued. Then place your hands on your abdomen, your hara, and close your legs. Open your eyes when ready. This should take 15 minutes or more.

HEALING WITH SOUND

It is fashionable to use didgeredoo, tibetan bowls and different instruments or tuning forks for each chakra. Your voice can do the same. With sound, much as a dolphin, you can detect any blocks in the body by slowly sending it to another and when you come to a sticky bit you tone into it. Or you can use sound on the chakras. The precision of the right note for a chakra can be intuitive or can be dowsed for. As you tone into each chakra you can imagine or verbalise that a colour is being poured into it. Each planet and astrological sign has a tone and can be utilised to heal a persons character. (See Sacred Sounds (Transformation through Music and Word) by Ted Andrews, Llewellyn Publications, ISBN 0-87542-018-4).

As time goes on, you find that your voice produces more and more overtones audibly. It is believed that the human voice has many more overtones and natural power than any other instrument. You do not have to be a musician to use your voice for healing.

Every sound, musical or not, has overtones - these are vibrations set in motion at the same time as the primary tone. For example, if the note of middle C is struck upon the piano, the strings for the note of G above middle C, E, B flat and so on begin to vibrate. Four or five overtones are normally detectable and recognised in music, but the overtones extend much further than the human ear can detect.

MANTRAS

Sacred Sounds used in Meditation and Chanting

Man = mind   Tra = protection and instrument

Meditation, chanting, and similar techniques increase the coherence and harmony in the brainwave patterns: they bring greater balance between hemispheres, which suggests that higher order and harmony is achieved.

OM	Totality of sound and existence - a calling signal to other beings of Light - O masculine M feminine - release and harmonise
AUM (AhOhMm)	Enhances visualisation - thoughts become more crystallised - attracts energies from subtle planes - repairs and builds
OM MANI PADME HUM	The jewel in the lotus - link to Goddess Kwan Yin - link to crown chakra and finite within the infinite
AMEN	So be it - primal parent
AMEN-RA	Divine producer of life - true essence of male and female
HU	Sufi word for He - the Father God

EHEIEH Hebrew Qabala - I am that I am - life breath in all (Eh-Heh-Yeh) things

SEVEN CHAKRA SEED SOUNDS AND VOWEL SOUNDS
LAM   VAM   RAM   SAM, YAM   HAM   OM   -
O (rope), OO (due), AH (father), AY(play), EE (see), MM, NN, NGNG

OM NAMAH SHIVAYA
  In the name of Shiva

OM AH HUM Great power to purify atmosphere prior to ritual or meditation and to transmute material offering to their spiritual counterparts

NAMYO HO REN GE KYO
  Buddhist - Infinite Miraculous Law of the Lotus Flower - Sutra or The Miraculous Order of the Infinite Universe - energises physical and mental

SU For harmonisation in peace for us and others - closing and grounding

ISIS, ASTARTE, DIANA, HECATE, DEMETER, KALI, INANNA
  Pagan Goddess Chant

THE EARTH, THE WATER, THE FIRE, AND THE AIR RETURN, RETURN, RETURN for ritual chant and casting a circle

and many more...

EXERCISES

✏ Chant on these vowel sounds in this order AIEOU (AhIi(as in pick)EhOhOOh). This according to Chinese philosophy, is the order of vowel resonance for perfect harmony in the New Age coming, each vowel having a specific meaning related to the mental, physical and spiritual state.

✏ Find a piece of paper and pencil. Close your eyes, and chant on each vowel separately. Draw the pattern each vowel makes in your perception. Then stand up and move your arms to each vowel and then finally move your arms to the shape your arms make. If you feel your name does not resonate with you think about changing it.

✏ Chant on the Om sound and send it to anyone who needs absent healing. Send it to specific parts of the body necessary or to the person as a whole. Sound travels.

✏ In a group situation sit in a circle and place a person in the middle lying down or sitting. Open your hearts, send sounds to this person as a group. Sense the sound the person needs like a dolphin using sonar. The low notes seem to hit the lower part of the body and the higher notes the higher parts. You will find the group becomes a choir and the energy in the room becomes very refined and beautiful - many times angels are felt. You will find the person in the middle receives a lot of energy and healing.

MOVEMENT TO MUSIC

Dancing and rhythm are almost essential to feeling whole. Rhythms can energise and stimulate our basic primal energies and it said percussion instruments activate the lower chakras. These are linked to the adrenals and kidneys and our basic life force and also our sexuality - the physical expression of our dynamic spiritual vitality. Dance every day.

Slow movements for each chakra to beautiful slow music such as the choir on Passion by Peter Gabriel, can centre you in a few minutes. Use these movements in succession.

- BASE CHAKRA - swing hands at hips and sway body

- ABDOMEN CHAKRA - hold hands up at 45 degree angle towards head and sway body

- SOLAR PLEXUS - hold hands straight up above head and sway body

- HEART CHAKRA - hold hands out from heart and swing out to shoulder height and back and sway body

- THROAT CHAKRA - push hands forward from throat to arms stretch and round and back to throat and sway body

- THIRD EYE - hold hands in prayer above head and sway body

- CROWN CHAKRA - open hands and arms wide to heaven and sway body

Repeat sequence until the end of the music.

Move your body to the rhythm of life and be free.

Don't forget that sound has memory link and can bring back this life and past lives - find your own chants to remember your past - have fun!

BREATHING

The following breathing exercises are based on Ancient Far Eastern knowledge. Each breath should be done six to ten times. Do not rush them or do them at all once. Do them all at a comfortable speed spread out over a week if necessary.

It is advisable that we maintain a breathing pattern that is slow, deep and long rather than fast, shallow and short. Make sure you are always breathing into your abdomen, and not above it without raising your shoulders. Your physical, mental and spiritual development are reflected in the way you breath. You do not consciously listen to your breathing all the time, it should just happen naturally. If you are eating a healthy well balanced diet this automatically helps your breathing.

Very slow, quiet and long breathing for selflessness

This breathing is done through the nose inhaling and exhaling very quietly. The out breath is 2 to 3 times longer than the in breath.

This calms all physical, mental and spiritual activities, so we enter deep meditation, and to develop inner sight, minimising egocentric delusion.

Normal slow and quiet breathing for harmony

This breathing is also done through the nose and is slightly stronger than above. This is for a time of stillness and the out breath is 2 to 3 times longer than the in breath.

This is to maintain peaceful, harmonious relations with actively moving surroundings, keeping centred which increases awareness of our surroundings.

Slow and quiet but stronger breathing for confidence

This breath is inhaled through the nose and exhaled through the slightly opened mouth. The exhalation is 3 to 5 times longer than the inhalation. It is stronger than the first two breaths.

It accelerates active harmony among all physical, mental, and spiritual functions by developing inner confidence, to adapt to any change in environment.

Long, deep, strong breathing for action

This breath is done through slightly opened mouth for both inhaling and exhaling. The exhalation is 3 to 5 times longer than the duration of inhalation.

This activates all physical, mental and spiritual powers to do anything without losing objective observation. It can release physical and mental stagnation, producing relaxation

Long, deep, strong and powerful breathing, with sound for spiritualisation

This breath is done through the mouth for both inhaling and exhaling. The exhalation is 3 to 5 times longer than the inhalation. Breath in HI and exhale FU.

This actively energises the physical and mental metabolism and spiritualises the entire personality.

Breathing with the hara for physicalisation

This breath is done through the nose deeply and slowly with natural movement of the hara or central region of the abdomen. When filling with breath, it naturally expands and naturally contracts on the out breath. Between inhalation and exhalation the breath should be held for several seconds. The exhalation should be generally 2 or 3 times longer than the inhalation.

This generates physical energy, mental stability, and spiritual confidence. It also produces an increase in body temperature, accelerates active digestive and circulatory functions for total health and longevity.

Breathing with the centre of the stomach region for power

This breath is done with natural movement in the region of the stomach. At the time of inhalation the stomach region naturally expands toward the outside, and at the time of exhalation, it contracts. Between the inhalation and exhalation the breath should be held for several seconds. The duration of exhalation is slightly longer than the duration of inhalation.

The effect of this breathing is the development of endurance, patience, and tolerance, and when the breath is held for a long time between inhalation and exhalation, it intensifies internal energisation throughout the whole body, so that the body is filled with spiritual power or electromagnetic energy. As a result, this breathing results in the development of various physical and mental abilities.

Breathing with the heart region for love

In this breathing both the inhalation and exhalation are slow and long, concentrating in the heart region, or the central region of the upper chest. The duration of inhaling is almost equal to the duration of exhaling, and the breath is not held between inhaling and exhaling - both naturally and smoothly continue in slow, long movements.

The effect of this breathing is to harmonise the beating of the heart and to generate smooth circulation of the blood and other body fluids. Mentally it generates a feeling of harmony and love with all aspects of the environment and people. It also develops sensitivity, sympathy, understanding and compassion.

Breathing with the region of the throat and the root of the tongue for intelligence

This breathing is done at the region of the throat and root of the tongue, with stronger inhaling and weaker exhaling. At the time of inhaling, the breath is concentrated and held at the throat and root of the tongue for several seconds and released.

The effect of this breathing is to develop keen senses for physical and mental concentration toward a certain objective. It further develops clear observation and penetrating insight into a problem being faced. Spiritual concentration is accelerated and intellectual comprehension is stimulated.

Breathing with the region of the midbrain for spiritualisation

This breathing is done at the region of the midbrain, the inner centre of the head. The inhalation is made slowly but sharply, as if breathing up toward the zenith of the head, with the feeling of lifting the body upward. This inhalation should be made smoothly and continuously, as long as possible, and at its extreme point the breath is suddenly but gently released. The exhalation should be made downward toward the mouth.

The effect of this breathing is to spiritualise our relative consciousness toward a more universal scope, and it further serves to release our perception into boundless dimensions, including the understanding of events taking place at a distance and telepathy. The entire physical metabolism rapidly slows down as this breathing is repeatedly exercised and body temperature decreases.

You can use the above methods in daily life while sitting, working or being active.

PLANETS AND ASTROLOGY

The following lists are references to help you understand your natal chart, a little more.

Planets rule an astrological sign which sits in one of twelve houses in the chart. The chart represents what is happening from earth.

The twelve house sections are basically thirty degrees each for every sign. The central dot represents us personally on earth. The Ascendant, begins the first house, representing the Eastern horizon as it intersects the ecliptic. From the earth the ecliptic appears as the sun's path around the earth in a year. The Descendant is 180 degrees opposite the Ascendant.

The Midheaven, or MC or Medium Coeli, begins the tenth house, representing the meridian as it intersects the ecliptic. The meridian is a great circle on the celestial sphere (projection of the earth to plot co-ordinates) passing through North and South points of the horizon and Earth, directly above the observer.

The Cusp Line begins each of the twelve signs and houses. There are four elements of Fire, Earth, Air, and Water and three temperaments Cardinal, Fixed and Mutable starting from Aries as Fire and Cardinal, then Taurus as Earth and Fixed and so on in order around the chart. There are also positive and negative signs starting with Aries as positive, Taurus as negative and so on. In a chart there needs to be a balance of elements, temperaments and positive and negative flow.

KEYWORDS

FOUR ELEMENTS

{FIRE	Intuitive, positive, aggressive, creative, masculine
{EARTH	Sensory, practicality
{AIR	Intellectual, communication, inter-relationships
{WATER	Sensitivity, intuition, psychic aspects, depth

THREE TEMPERAMENTS

{CARDINAL	Active, direct, decisive, expansive, motivation, thoughtless
{FIXED	Stubborn, inflexible, cautious, persistent, determined, rigid
{MUTABLE	Easy going, adaptable, willing to change, experiences changes

{POSITIVE	Flow, energy, outgoing, masculine, aggressive,
{NEGATIVE	Ingoing, feminine, ebb, passive, attracting desires

A planet can appear in its own house and sign as Mars in Aries in the first house, or Mars can be placed in any other sign and any other house. When this occurs, correlate the meaning of the planet with the meaning of the sign and then the meaning of the particular house it is in. This is how you begin to understand your own chart and placements of planets in sign and house.

With practice you can become an expert!

✩✩✩

1ST HOUSE - The self, the ways you do and respond to things
SIGN - ARIES - "I am", impulsive, self centred, give up easily, initiator, head
PLANET RULER - MARS - male, active, aggressive, motivation, sexual energy, danger

✩✩✩

2ND HOUSE - Self with security and feelings, through money, possessions and anything material relating to the individual
SIGN - TAURUS - "I have", cautious, stubborn, good living, collector of things, practical, determined, throat
PLANET RULER - VENUS - love of beautiful things and material needs

✩✩✩

3RD HOUSE - Communication with the self, confined to short distances, close exchanges with people - sisters, brothers, neighbours, all forms of movement to collect and exchange information and express the self
SIGN - GEMINI - "I think", fluidity, optimistically, unreservedly, mentality, versatility, non-conformism, shoulders, lungs, arms, wrists, hands
PLANET RULER - MERCURY - mind, mentality, information, travelling, communication

✩✩✩

4TH HOUSE - Home, to do with the mother, childhood, private life, unconscious drives
SIGN - CANCER - "I feel", emotionally, protectively, imitatively, sensitivity, domesticity, tenacity, stomach, abdomen, breasts, womb
PLANET RULER - MOON - emotions, maternal feelings, attitudes from family in childhood, reaction to external influences, relationship to other women, eating habits, food preferences

✿✿✿

*5TH HOUSE - Self expression, self representation, act of creating another human being, parenthood (especially fatherhood), artistic creativity which is a projection of self in a variety of symbolic forms

<u>SIGN - LEO</u> - "I will", ostentatiously, proudly, vitality, authority, power, heart, spine, mid-back

<u>PLANET RULER - SUN</u> - vitality, self expression, outer self, creative energies, express of will

✿✿✿

*6TH HOUSE - Work and health, illnesses, physical weaknesses and strengths

<u>SIGN -VIRGO</u> - "I analyse", analytical, watchful, reservedly, timidly, discrimination, methodical, nurse, being in service, intestines, appendix

<u>PLANET RULER - MERCURY</u> - mind, mental, analyse

and CHIRON - new healing energy, spiritual awakening, healing old wounds

✿✿✿

*7TH HOUSE - Self and other people, one-to-one relationships to and with other people

<u>SIGN - LIBRA</u> - "I balance", sensual, gentle, harmony, companionships, indecisive, lower back

<u>PLANET RULER - VENUS</u> - social and aesthetic values, emotions in relationships

✿✿✿

*8TH HOUSE - Hidden factors, unconscious desires, secrets, death and afterlife

<u>SIGN - SCORPIO</u> - "I desire", determinedly, intensely, regeneration, resourceful, secrecy, reproductive system

<u>PLANET RULER - PLUTO</u> - transformation, regeneration, hidden strength, permanent change, upheaval for human life and civilisations

✪✪✪

*9TH HOUSE - Deeper meanings of life and expresses individual's type of philosophy and religious beliefs, long distance travel, language, foreign cultures
<u>SIGN - SAGITTARIUS</u> - "I see", enthusiastically, philosophically, tactlessly, aspiration, exploration, thighs, last vertebrae, buttocks
<u>PLANET RULER - JUPITER</u> - self expansion, attaining wisdom, karmic rewards, compassion, generosity to less fortunate

✪✪✪

*10TH HOUSE - Ambition, type of image an individual shows to the outside world, the conscious drives
<u>SIGN - CAPRICORN</u> - "I use", seriously, detached, pessimistically, ambition, conservatism, conscientiousness, organisation, skeletal, knees, skin, nails, hair
<u>PLANET RULER - SATURN</u> - Restriction, responsibility, careers, lessons to learn, difficulties, limitations

✪✪✪

*11TH HOUSE - Groups, societies, clubs, friends, acquaintances, establishing new and sometimes revolutionary order to benefit humanity
<u>SIGN - AQUARIUS</u> - "I know", eccentricity, radically, reactionary, humanitarian, independent, originality, ankles, calves, blood circulation
<u>PLANET RULER - URANUS</u> - change, trauma, destroying old for a better new, freedom, individuality, link to universe for original ideas, purpose of soul and more karmic freedom to express creativity

✪✪✪

*12TH HOUSE - All that is hidden, the unconscious, selfless action and motivation, psychic and psychological forms and ideas, ideals, institutions, prisons, hospitals

<u>SIGN - PISCES</u> - "I believe", dreamy, unconsciously, absent mindedly, compassion, renunciation, universality, feet, water retention

<u>PLANET RULER - NEPTUNE</u> - Ideals, unconscious, intuitive, creative, universal love

PLANETS IN ASPECT
Degrees

0-5	Conjunct	emphasises planets
60	Sextile	opportunities
90	Square	blocks within
120	Trine	good fortune
180	Opposition	conflict, problem with others

RECOMMENDED ASTROLOGY BOOKS

To further your knowledge in setting up and reading charts the following books are very worthwhile for your progress:

The American Ephemeris by Ned F Michelson
(ACS Publishers)
Time Changes in the World by Doris Chase Doane
(American Federation of Astrologers)
Phillip's World Atlas
Raphael's Table of Houses of Great Britain of Northern Latitudes
(Foulsham)
The Astrologer's Handbook by Francis Sakoian and Louis S Acker
(Penguin)
Martin Schulman:
(Samuel S Weiser)
Celestial Harmony
Karmic Astrology   - The Moon's Nodes and Reincarnation
                               - Retrogrades and Reincarnation
                               - Joy and the Part of Fortune

PART THREE

WHEN YOU ARE A HEALER

It is totally advisable to be part of a healing circle or development group such as the ones I run.

They should show you how to work on the aura, chakras and hands on healing. Find a recommended teacher only and with whom you feel totally comfortable with if possible. There are many different wavelengths and many approaches. We also change wavelength as we grow so do not worry if you outgrow your teacher - it is just time to move on.

In the UK it is also advisable to become a probationary member of a member group of the CHO to become insured.

You should learn about the chakras and aura which is basically made up of the etheric (physical layer), astral (emotional layer), mental (thought layer) and spiritual layer. Our aura is usually seen as about three feet wide and this can spread if you are opening as a channel for Universal Love and Light. Some people can see clairvoyantly the chakras and colours in the aura. Again it is strongly advisable to go on a recommended colour healing course to become specifically a colour healer.

Colours seen in the aura can mean the following but I recommend that you formulate your own ideas as time goes on from the many systems used today.

COLOURS SEEN IN AURA

MAROON	Moving into ones task
RED	Passion, strong feelings
Rose Pink	unconditional love
Clear red	moving anger
Dark red	stagnated anger
Red-orange	sexual passion
ORANGE	Ambition
YELLOW	Intellect
GREEN	Healing, healer, nurturer
BLUE	Teacher, sensitivity
PURPLE	Deeper connection to spirit
INDIGO	Moving toward a deeper connection to spirit
LAVENDER	Spirit
WHITE	Truth
GOLD	Connection to God, in the service of humankind, Godlike love
SILVER	Communication
BLACK	Absence of light, or profound forgetting, thwarted ambition (cancer)
BLACK VELVET	Like black holes in space, doorways to other realities

COLOURS USED IN HEALING

RED — Charging the field, burning out cancer, warming cold areas
(NEVER USE TOO MUCH RED as it effects the nervous system quickly)
PINK — Soothing, unconditional love
ORANGE — Charging the field, increasing sexual potency, increasing immunity
YELLOW — Charging third chakra, clearing a foggy head
GREEN — Charging fourth chakra, balancing, general healing, charging field
BLUE — Cooling, calming, restructuring etheric level, shielding
PURPLE — Connecting to spirit
INDIGO — Opening third eye, clearing head
LAVENDER — Purging field
WHITE — Charging field, bring peace and comfort, taking away pain
GOLD — Restructuring outer layer of aura, strengthening field, charging field
SILVER — Strong purging of field
VELVET BLACK — Bringing patient into a state of grace, silence and peace with God
PURPLE BLACK — Taking away pain when doing deep tissue work and work on bone cells, helping expand patients field in order to connect to their purpose

As healers, we always have our own lessons and continue to develop throughout our life to improve our work and understanding of self. We should try to draw in as much worthwhile information as possible and attend as many seminars, talks and workshops as necessary. Also we become more discerning as to who we choose to listen to. We can learn from every single person we meet. We take what we need and discard the rest. There are many people in the New Age on an ego trip and trying to make a quick buck - BEWARE! Also beware of teachers who dominate you and do not allow you your individualism within reason or space to meet other teachers or groups. As we are working with an unseen world it is very easy to have many points of view and also to exaggerate or even make believe there is a guide with you or your aura is bright orange for instance. PLEASE BE CAREFUL.

Monitoring your own progress also means watching your own ego so that it does not get in the way. It is a good idea to check your motives for becoming a healer - is it your need to be needed that is satisfied?

You must check you are working for the best intentions for your patient and are channelling the purest energy with the highest vibrations that you are capable of carrying at that time. You need to create and hold the right atmosphere and environment for healing with some relaxation music such as tapes composed by me or other New Age companies. There are a variety of tapes now on the market such as dolphin and whale sounds, nature sounds and so on.

You must never say you can cure a patient. You are there to help them towards healing themselves and you work as a catalyst. You can give them some form of meditation or visualisation to do every day. Healthy diet and drinking at least three pints of water a day is very important.

Patients should not rely on you totally to heal them, and you must try to have detached involvement. This is even more important when you are seeing client after client. How can you carry their problems? It is definitely not professional to talk about your problems or other patients problems during a session.

You must try to be aware of using Universal energy and not your own energy. You must learn to ask for Gods will to be done and not your own; in so doing, keeping your ego aside and allowing the patient to receive what they need.

If you are picking up that your client has a serious illness you must always recommend them to go to their doctor. If you receive any messages at all say them afterwards if you think they are totally relevant. Healing energy is NOT the same as clairvoyant energy although the two come hand in hand in your development at times. Do not tell your patient anything worrying such as they have a life threatening disease, or their husband is going to die. Do not let your ego or so called guidance make you think you are always right without a second opinion from another professional such as a GP. You must be totally tactful and thoughtful.

Be sensitive to the patients needs and make sure they are comfortable. The session is for them and not for you. Tune into the healing vibration before the patient arrives through meditation. If you cannot deal with the patient suggest another practitioner. Do not expect to help everyone.

Remember illness first enters the auric field before the body but often people leave it too late. Learn some simple anatomy and about illnesses.

Tell the patient how you heal and put their mind at rest about everything.

The most important part is to allow them to relax and trust you. You may feel hot or cold energy from hands. Hot tends to be putting in energy, cold is taking out negativity. The patients eyelids may flicker as in rapid eye movement, due to the relaxation. They often look younger as their anxiety is relieved. Many people have not relaxed in that way for a long time or if ever.

Always listen as so much of communication is listening. Give empathy but not sympathy. Help the patient to take responsibility for their life and perhaps if appropriate, their illness - and therefore their healing process. Be positive without being dogmatic. There often is not a solution to the problem - your role is simply to listen. Suggest a book or class or other practitioner when necessary, but do not bombard them with information. You are there to show them the way. If you find there is no improvement or proof that they are helping themselves in four sessions you need to ask them to think about what they are not doing and that they may be wasting their time and money. Are they using their illness as a prop for attention? This can be the case at times.

Remember to close the patient down to be in their bodies as you have heightened their vibration and they are not used to that. You can close their chakras down in your mind and ask them to put a bubble of white light around them imagining no holes in the bubble. Ground them with roots growing over their feet. Allow them time to come back into the room slowly and don't let them get up too quickly after the session. A lot has taken place on a subconscious level as well as auric level. They need time to centre themselves.

Sometimes pain can be increasingly worse for a few days as it is coming out of the body and thus leaving the body. This should be explained as being normal. Also they may need to sleep as soon as they get home as part of their healing.

Be sure to clean your aura and even the room after they have left. You can close down your chakras, or wipe off unwanted energies from your body, wash your hands or light a candle with a prayer - whatever you are comfortable with.

Remember, above all, to take care of yourself and maintain your channel with regular meditation, discipline, dealing with your own issues, receiving regular healing, having a good diet, exercising, and don't forget to laugh and have play time. You do not have to be a complete saint to be a healer!!

Always acknowledge and recognise your own stages of development and be kind to yourself by allowing this growth process. You may become more sensitive as you become more aware of higher energies. You may become allergic to certain foods. You may need more rest and even may need to stop healing for a while.

BASIC CHAKRA HEALING TECHNIQUE

Preferably find a quiet and conducive space with some soothing music in the background. Sit your client in a chair with their back to you. Explain the healing process and that you may or may not touch them at different chakra points. You can firstly dowse with your pendulum on each chakra to see if there are any energy blocks. You will find your own spin for negative or positive and if it begins to spin the wrong way or be still, there are difficulties in this area and associated psychology, glands and organs. (See Hands of Light by Barbara Ann Brennan for detailed spins of pendulum) Also check for any pain or blocks elsewhere in the body - if the pendulum swings there is a block. After the session the pendulum should swing well on the chakras and be still on any other blocks in the body.

Place your hands on the patients shoulders and tune into the Light to pour through and to give the patient what they need. Say a continuous prayer mentally during this whole process. Start at the crown chakra and work your way down through each chakra. You can work on the aura or hands on. Then, go to any other areas of the body that need healing. Never touch the patient near very sensitive sexual areas.

This should last 20 to 30 minutes. Always close the patients chakras down and ground them and yourself too. This may be the first time they have opened their awareness and spin of their chakras. Just remember how sensitive you are in meditation and put yourself in their shoes. You can end by saying "God Bless and just open your eyes when you are ready feeling that your feet are very firmly rooted to the earth". Then wait for your patient to awaken slowly. Always ask how they are feeling. Discuss what has taken place and show them with the pendulum that the healing has improved their chakra spin and that the healing has gone through any difficult spots.

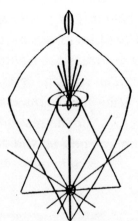

MAY LOVE AND LIGHT ALWAYS BE WITH YOU

RETURN TO LOVE

Remembering your Source is not enough. Talking New Age language is not enough. If you do not walk your talk there is not much point in knowing the Truth. If you end up with egocentric dillusion and live in your own fantasy, there is not much you are doing to help your fellow man and this planet.

If you stand outside your Truth you are not sharing your Wisdom. If you become absorbed with outside karma you have lost your centre and focus. If you are dogmatic in your viewpoint you will cause friction with others. If you do not link to the wisdom of Natural Law you are not synchronising with Truth.

If you do not see your weaknesses, especially in the areas of greed, jealousy and power, you are not truly honest. If you are not honest to self, you are not to others. If you cannot truly love yourself, you will never know how to truly love others.

You can only give of yourself truly when you are not expecting reward, and when you know that the fulfilment of giving is more reward than any thing given in return.

How is it that the purity of giving is lost in a haze of wanting some thing back? How is it that true loving is lost in the need of some thing? How is it that great men of Truth are so few on this Earth? Where is devotion to heal others and selflessness? Have human failings always to step in and deny good relationships with others? Have human life-form got the capacity to always take care of each other and this planet?

To rebuild our planet and our relationship to one another and all of Nature, we must be unconditional, unselfish and have a sincere heart. Love is the key.

We must return to Love.

FURTHER READING

Loving Relationships I and II by Sondra Ray
(Celestial Arts)
Toning by Laurel Elizabeth Keyes
(DeVorss)
Wheels of Life by Anodea Judith
(Llewellyn)
Hands of Light by Barbara Ann Brennan
(A Banham New Age Book)
Man's Eternal Quest by Paramahansa Yogananda
(Self Realisation Fellowship)
Sacred Sounds by Ted Andrews
(Llewellyn)
Wisdom from White Eagle
(White Eagle Lodge Publishing Trust)
Cymatics by Hans Jenny
(Basilius Press)
An Ascension Handbook by Tony Stubbs
(Oughten House)
Eastern Light Magazine - Pat Palgrave Moore
Tel: 01643 611386
Seeds of Light Magazine - Heather Adamson
Tel: 01945 583835

RECOMMENDED COURSES

The Atkinson Ball College of Hypnotherapy - Tel: 01704 576285
The Call of an Angel Courses - Tel: 0181 550 4122

MUSIC

Seventh Wave Music - 01822 880301
Bands of Gold - 0181 550 4122